Lock Down Publications and Ca$h
Presents

Thug of Spades 2
The Deepest Cut

Written By
Corey Robinson

First Edition 2023

Printed in the United States of America

This is a work of fiction. Names, characters, places, and incidents either are products of the author's imagination or are used fictitiously. Any similarity to actual events or locales or persons, living or dead, is entirely coincidental.

Lock Down Publications
P.O. Box 944
Stockbridge, GA 30281
www.lockdownpublications.com

Like our page on Facebook: Lock Down Publications
www.facebook.com/lockdownpublications.ldp

Stay Connected with Us!

Text **LOCKDOWN** to 22828 to stay up-to-date with new releases, sneak peaks, contests and more…

Like our page on Facebook:
Lock Down Publications

Join Lock Down Publications/The New Era Reading Group

Visit our website:
www.lockdownpublications.com

Follow us on Instagram:
Lock Down Publications

Email Us: We want to hear from you!

PROLOGUE

"Sup, Day? Nigga, you 'bout ready for that sweet taste of freedom?" Mellow asked when he walked inside of Daymion's cell.

Daymion Myers had done seventeen long years in the belly of the beast and was scheduled for release in less than twenty four hours. To say that he wasn't a little skittish would be a lie but he was ready for the next chapter of his life to begin even if he wasn't sure how his story would end.

"Shit, freedom and pussy. Nigga, you know I'm ready for that. Been too mufuckin' long without it, but my number one priority is going to be Dre. I got to get out there and save him before he fucks around and let's those damn streets suck him completely in. I don't want him to turn out like me. I want my lil nigga to be greater than that."

"Yeah, dawg, I know just what you saying but don't you think you might be a little too late for that? Shit is running through his veins, Day, and you know as well as I do that once you get a little taste of that dish the streets serve up, it's all you wanna eat."

Daymion gave Mellow an angry look but he knew that he was right because when his brother Trey gave him his first bite of the game, he stayed hungry for more. There was nothing else that he could think of that he would have rather done with his life. But hitting the streets and stacking paper was the fuck up. However, that type of life was not what he wanted for his son. He couldn't believe that Kiara had forced

Dre to go out like that. He needed someone to guide him. Day just hoped he wasn't too late.

A life in the streets led to two things, death or prison and he didn't want Dre to have to experience either one. He wondered just how much damage Kiara had already done to his mind. He had been happy when Kayla brought him for a visit but it only happened once. The next time she came and he wasn't with her, Daymion already knew why.

"Ya know Mellow, I wanted my boy to finish school and possibly even go to college. Be a fucking pro athlete or something like that. Man, my son will be a grown man soon but he ain't supposed to be out there like that. He should be finessing the ladies and figuring out who he's going to take to the prom not pushing dope for a nothing ass nigga like Dory."

"Shit Day, I ain't even gonna lie. My pops had me out there at twelve years old putting in work like a grown ass man and once my pockets started getting laced up, I didn't want to stop. That shit was like the greatest high I'd ever had and the bitches throw the pussy to you all day as long as the paper is right. You know that feeling too."

"I know what you saying Mell because they started me out young too, but look at all the street life has cost us. My brother is dead and gone and I'm locked the fuck up because of a bitch who made me believe she was grown. My fucking dick got me in a situation I never saw coming and if I wouldn't have been in those damn streets, I would have never got caught up with her ass."

"Nah mane, that shit could have happened regardless. You can't blame everything that goes down on the game because we chose it, not the other way around. It ain't the streets fault. Sometimes, we just gotta suck it up and take responsibility for our own actions. We made the decision to do what we did. We just happened to be a part of the game when we did it."

Daymion knew that Mellow was talking some real nigga shit and he had to agree that it was his own fuck ups that had cost him. If he wouldn't have been weak for a pretty face and some good pussy, he would have never lost more than seventeen years of his life. The only good that came of it was Dreighton and he made all that Daymion had been through well worth it.

"You know what Mell? You bout the realest nigga I ever met and I give you my word that I'm a hold you down when I bounce, and I'm a be right out front when you walk out so your ass better be ready."

"Nigga, I stay ready. Just don't take your ass out there and play Superman. I know that's your seed but you can't go out there and make demands on the little nigga. Shit, that's what his momma did. Just go out there and be a father and teach him how to be a man and then let him choose his future. He'll respect you more if you lead and let him decide if he wants to follow. Don't force it."

Daymion couldn't help but respect what Mellow had told him because he knew he had no right to go out there and try to run shit in anyone's life. Whatever Dre decided he wanted to do, he would have his back and dared a mufucka to touch him.

Chapter 1

"Come on Dory, just a few more steps and then you can rest."

"Nah, fuck that. I can't do this shit no more. That bitch should have just killed me because there's no way I can keep living like this."

"Why would you say some shit like that? You're still young and have so much to live for. Besides, the doctor said that all of this is only temporary. You've been doing so much better with the rehabilitation and now you're taking more steps. You'll be up and moving around on your own in no time."

Dory looked up at Kaprice like she had lost her mind. He couldn't believe what she'd said because she wasn't in his position. How could she have possibly known what he was going through? True enough, she had stepped up to the plate and stuck by him after he'd been shot. She helped him through all of the physical therapy and everything else in between but she couldn't feel his pain or even imagine it. Dory felt less and less of a man with each day that passed and often times contemplated ending his miserable existence, but he just could never get the nerve up to go through with it.

"Bitch. The fuck is you talking about? I can't even feel my dick right now. My black ass can't do shit but lay in the bed or sit in this fuckin' wheelchair. It's a struggle to even wipe my own ass. You think I want to depend on someone else to clean the shit outta my ass crack for the rest of my life? What type of life is that for a nigga like me?"

Kaprice often tried to grapple with what Dory was going through, but deep inside, she knew that there was no way she could understand. She had never been shot before and she couldn't even imagine being temporarily paralyzed but she did have to put up with Dory's bitching and complaining. The shit had started to get old but she tried to hang in there and stay by his side. She hoped that it would one day pay off. She had always wanted to be his main chick but he never let her get past side bitch status. She wanted to be more than a piece of pussy to him but started to wonder if it was even worth the headache.

Dory told her, "You was aching to be my bitch, so here you go." She knew that he would fuck her up if she strayed. She remembered when she had first got with Dory. He spent grands finessing her and pulling her into his web and as soon as he realized he had her, all the spoiling faded away slowly. He brought Shay into the picture and it was as if she no longer existed but look what Shay had done to him. He couldn't even bend Kaprice over and dick her down anymore and that seemed to make him resent her even more and pushed them far apart.

Kaprice had thought about laying down with the next baller but she was too afraid that Dory would find out. She smiled at the thought of having a man deep inside of her but the thought didn't last long because Dory brought her back to reality.

"Aye, I'm a need you to take a ride over to Gun's and pick up that package he has for me."

"Why can't he just bring it over here? He's been dropping it off. What makes this time any different?"

"Bitch, who the hell is you to question what I tell you to do? Now take your ass over there and pick up my shit, and don't take all day."

Kaprice smacked her lips and rolled her eyes and then grabbed the car keys that hung on the hook by the door. She had grown sick of Dory talking to her like a piece of shit but knew that if she didn't follow his instructions, there would be hell to pay. He may have been unable to use his legs but his fists still worked just fine and he didn't mind raising them. Kaprice went to bed many nights with a black eye and busted lip. She hated being treated that way but she didn't have the heart to leave Dory to fend for himself. She seemed to be all that he had left.

He leaned on her heavily when he found out about Malice being shot and she thought it had brought them closer but once the grieving process was over, he was back to being his old self. She often wished that she would have never come to his rescue but she had been so lonely and so desperate for a man's touch and didn't realize the mistake she had made until it was too late.

She pulled in to Big Gun's driveway and slowly got out. The cool breeze felt good against her cocoa colored skin so she stood for a minute up against the car and took it all in. In the back of her mind, she still wondered why she had to make the pick up because Gun always moved his own product and cash. However, she didn't have time to worry about it because all she wanted to do was handle business and be gone. She had no reason to stay any longer than she had to. She finally let out a long breath and walked up the short concrete path that led to Gun's front door and rang the bell. It felt like it took forever for him to answer it but when he finally did, Kaprice was thrown completely off guard.

Gun stood in front of her shirtless with his diamond encrusted Jesus piece hanging on a platinum chain that dripped from his neck. Her eyes trailed his torso and followed the lines of every tattoo that adorned it. She knew that she should look away but her eyes betrayed her and stayed focused on his form. When her vision traveled down a little further, she couldn't help but notice the print in his sweatpants. It felt like it had been forever since she had felt a man's touch and she just couldn't help herself.

"You just gon' stand there and look at my dick or you gon' bring yo' ass inside?"

"Oh my God, Gun, I am so sorry. I didn't mean to stare. I just. I'm so sorry."

Gun smiled and grabbed his thick manhood, "Nah ma, don't be sorry. I know that nigga ain't been giving you what you need. That's why I asked him to send you over here. I'm trying to give you what you been missing at home. Some good dick."

"I thought fucking your partner's woman was off limits. Ain't that one of the rules you street thugs are supposed to follow?"

"A nigga like me don't follow the rules and besides, this shit right here is gonna be just between us."

Kaprice folded her arms over her chest and began to back away from him. She wasn't scared of him, she just wondered what kind of game he was playing with her. "I thought you had Dory to send me over here to pick up a package, was that a lie?"

"Girl, just chill the fuck out. I'm a give you something to take back to the nigga but first. I'ma give you this dick. I know your ass needs something to make you feel good so come on and let a nigga do what he does best."

"You know what? Fuck you, Gun. I'm not doing this with you. I'm out of here!"

As soon as she said it, Gun stepped closer to her. Kaprice tried to move out of his way but he had her back against the wall and gave her nowhere to run. She was determined to resist him but when he slid his hand down the front of her shorts and found her swollen pearl, she knew there would be no turning back. She felt his long, thick finger enter her wetness and closed her eyes.

"Nah, open them mufuckas up. I wanna look in 'em when I make this pussy cum."

When he began to slide his finger in and out of her, thoughts she had held of Dory slowly faded away. "Uh, Gun, that feels so good."

"Yeah. You like that shit don't you?"

"Yes Gun, please don't stop."

He went against what she said and removed his finger. He didn't have time to stand there and play with her because he was ready to feel her wetness gush all over his manhood. "Turn around and face the wall. Let me give you the real deal."

Gun turned her toward the wall and slid her shorts and panties down to her ankles and she willingly stepped out of them. When he pulled his sweatpants down and stood against her, she could feel his hardness against the back of her thighs and opened her legs up naturally. She figured that since she had already crossed the line, why not go ahead and enjoy it? Gun palmed her medium sized ass and spread her cheeks. When the tip of his dick brushed against her back hole she flinched, "No Gun, I ain't never had nothing back there. That ain't my thing."

He smiled to himself and decided to get the pussy first and later on, he would venture into the backyard and break ground. He bent his knees slightly so he could be level with her and then pushed himself deep into her wetness. He closed his eyes and moaned in pleasure as soon as her tightness squeezed his dick. He could tell right away that she hadn't been fucked in a while.

"Mmm shit, no wonder Dory be keeping your ass in check."

No sooner than he said it, his cell phone rang. He was going to ignore the call but decided against it because it could have been a money making deal and he wasn't about

11

to miss out on any money for a piece of pussy. He had been deep on his grind lately because he was ready to build his own empire.

He pulled out mid stroke and caused Kaprice to turn around with a scowl on her face, "Come on Gun, it was just starting to feel good. Do you really have to take that call?"

Instead of giving her a verbal response, he pointed to the dining room table. She scrunched her eyebrows together as if she didn't understand what he told her. He saw her confusion, so to make clear what he wanted he walked over to the table and pulled out a chair and then sat in it so she could put in some work.

"Come on over here and ride this beast while I take this call."

Kaprice loved that freaky shit and secretly wished that one of his bitches was on the other end of the phone line because she had planned to put on one hell of a show. Gun licked his lips and watched his dick disappear as she slid down on top of it. He looked up and stared into her eyes and then answered his phone.

"Sup, my nigga? What can I do for you?"

"Yo Gun, where the hell is my bitch? Her ass should have been back by now."

Gun smiled and answered, "Nigga, she on my dick wettin' that mufucka up. Now I understand why you be keeping her ass locked up in the crib."

As soon as Kaprice realized that Gun was talking to Dory she tried to get off of him but he stopped her. "Na ma, you ain't got to get up. Keep riding this dick. I want this fuck nigga to hear them moans a real nigga gives you. Bitch nigga can't lay down no pipe to you right now so he might as well let someone else enjoy the pussy."

Dory couldn't believe that his right hand went and did some foul shit like that. He didn't put it past a bitch but him and Gun went way back and he thought their bond was solid.

"How the hell you gonna do some disloyal shit like that? That's my bitch and you know she off limits. The fuck is wrong with you nigga?"

"Ain't nobody trying to hear what you talking about you greedy ass mufucka. I done been through the war with you and had your back on everything. Our shit was supposed to be fifty fifty and then I find out you went behind my back and made a side deal to cut me out. Kind of fuck shit is that?"

"Aye mane, I was gonna put you up on it but I kept getting side tracked. You know I would never intentionally cut you out. When I eat, you eat and that ain't never gonna change but my bitch ain't got shit to do with what we got going on business wise."

"Your bitch? Nigga, this my bitch now. Your crippled ass aint' been giving her what she needs but I'm a put in that work. It took a real mufucka like me to make her feel special again but don't worry D, soon as I get this nut, I'm a send her back to ya, wet pussy and all."

Gun hit end call on his phone and lifted Kaprice up and sat her bare ass on the table top. She couldn't believe that he had sold her out like that and tried to get out of his hold. "Let me go you motherfucker. I can't believe you just did that shit. Do you have any idea of what Dory is going to do to me once I get home?"

"Bitch, you shoulda thought about that before you let me in this pussy. Now lay your ass back so I can finish what you started."

She couldn't believe that she had fallen for Gun's bullshit. She didn't even want to imagine what kind of wrath Dory was going to put on her once she went back to the house she stayed with him in. He might have been paralyzed from the waist down but he was still stronger than her. She lied there as still as she could while Gun pushed inside of her one final time and emptied his nut sack. She had never felt so

13

humiliated in her life. She lied there after he walked away and drowned in her own embarrassment. A loud thud on the table caused her to sit up quickly and when she did, she saw a thick manilla envelope on the table beside her.

"If you smart, you'll take that shit and get the hell outta dodge. You don't need that mufucka. Besides, stick around too long and you might just end up eating a dish that's meant for him."

Kaprice slowly reached over and picked up the envelope. She opened it and saw the neatly bundled stacks of hundred dollar bills and closed it back. She held it tightly to her chest and knew that Gun was right. She could either deliver the package to Dory and continue to live miserably or she could take the money and run. Maybe go somewhere and reinvent herself. She knew that once Dory completely healed, he would be done with her anyway, so she chose the latter option.

She got off the table and put her shorts back on. Fuck the panties, Gun's grimy ass could keep them. She ran out of his house and slammed the door behind her, just in case he changed his mind and tried to take the money back. When she started her car, she noticed the gas light on and gripped the steering wheel tightly. She knew that she wouldn't get far on what was in the tank so she decided to stop at the first gas station she saw.

She noticed that there were very few people at the Citgo so she pulled in. She was paranoid and felt like everyone was watching her so she grabbed the envelope full of money and put it in her purse and held it tightly in her grip. She was unsure of where her next destination would be but knew that she needed to put some distance between her and Dory. When she finished pumping her gas, she got a queasy feeling in the pit of her stomach and began to look around. She saw two young girls walk in the store giggling about something only known to them. An older couple sat at the pump next to her but it was nothing out of the ordinary. Kaprice opened her car door and got in so she could get the hell out of there. No sooner than she pushed her key in the ignition, she felt the cold hard steel pressed against her temple.

"You can have everything I got but please, just don't kill me. I'm not ready to die."

"Nah baby, it ain't what you got that I want. It's that nigga you been fucking with."

"I don't know what you're talking about."

"Oh yeah, you know just who the fuck I'm referring to. Ain't no sense in you playing dumb."

Daymion looked around the parking lot to make sure no one was paying him any attention and then turned back to Kaprice. "Move your ass over, I'm driving this bitch."

Kaprice didn't even try to argue. She went ahead and slid over to the passenger side so he could slide in. She felt her heart speed up and swore that she was about to have a heart attack. When the car pulled out of the parking lot, she turned her head and got a good look at the culprit. She couldn't believe that she was staring into the face of the infamous Daymion Myers.

"Oh my Gosh, Daymion. I thought you were locked up."

Kaprice remembered the days when Daymion was that nigga. All the bitches on the block had been sweating his nut sack, but he fucked around and let the wrong bitch get it in her hands, and it changed his life forever. She had always respected Daymion's gangsta and at that moment, she wasn't sure what to make of the situation at hand.

"I was locked up, but a nigga is free now and I got some shit I need to handle, so I need for you to tell me where that fuck nigga Dory living at."

"Please Daymion, you should really just forget about him and live your life. He ain't in a position to defend himself so consider that his karma."

Kaprice opened her purse and pulled out the manilla envelope Big Gun had given her. She dumped it out so Daymion could see all the cash, but little did she know, money was the last thing on his mind.

"The fuck kind of nigga you take me for? What? You think because I just stepped outta the pen and see some money I'm a jump and run off into the wind? Nah, that nigga gotta pay for thinking he can do my seed dirty. I was good to that nigga and he gon' disrespect my name. Hell no. I ain't letting that shit go. Now, tell me where to find him at."

Kaprice finally told him where Dory had been laying his head. He couldn't believe that nigga had the audacity to rest his head in his old territory.

"I can't go back there, Daymion. I just can't."

Daymion slowed the car down and pulled on to the side of the road so he could find out what kind of bullshit Kaprice was on. "I don't have time to pity your ass, you knew what kind of nigga he was and still chose to be with him. Now you gon' sit here and act like you scared. What's up with that?"

"He don't know where your son is at."

"The fuck you covering for that nigga for? If I remember correctly, he dissed you all those years ago for another nigga's bitch and yet, you still running behind him like a stray dog. The fuck is wrong with you?"

"I just wanted to take care of him. When he was shot, everyone turned their back on him and he needed somebody. I thought that it would make him respect me and one day love me but his ass is just as nasty to me as ever."

"It's all good and I ain't gonna make you go with me. He won't even know that I got the information from you so if you do decide to go back, you'll be aight. And don't worry, I ain't on no murder mission but I am gonna make him wish that I was."

"Daymion, you don't understand. Dory treats me like shit. At first, he was decent to me but over time, he started to change. He started putting his hands on me and talking to me as if I were dog shit on his shoes. After he got shot, he became worse than ever."

"Hold the fuck up. You keep talking about that nigga getting shot but I was in with his boy Mellow and he ain't mention nothing like that."

"Yeah, he cut Mellow off as soon as he got hemmed up. That's what Dory does when you're of no more use to him. That's probably why Mellow didn't say anything."

"Who the hell shot his grimy ass because I need to shake their hand."

"Well, besides me, he was fucking around with a young girl named Shay. Well, her and her brother Teddy took a liking to Dre and when they found out that Malice had been getting sent out there to try and rob him, they decided to rob Dory back. Shay would give Dre the money she stole from Dory and he would pay him with that. When he found out Shay was stealing from him, he beat her really bad. He even beat his baby out of her. She stayed in the hospital for a while and when Teddy showed up to avenge her, Dory killed him. When Shay was well enough to confront him, she took a gun with her and shot him in the back. I've been trying to help him get better ever since. He was temporarily paralyzed and I'm trying to help him walk again."

Daymion couldn't believe what he had heard. He had no clue about all that had happened to Dory but he knew it would give him a strong advantage over him.

"Ya ever heard of a nigga named Cardo?"

"Yeah, I heard of him but I don't know where to find him. They say he works for Malachi."

"Malachi Jensen?"

"That's the only Malachi I know and just to prepare you, he is Kiara's boyfriend too." Kaprice didn't know Malachi that well but she had heard of him. She couldn't give Daymion any more information and all she wanted to do was go somewhere safe because paralyzed or not, she was afraid Dory might find a way to look for her.

"Yeah, a nigga like that sounds like Kiara's style." Daymion could see the fear in Kaprice's eyes. He knew that she had nothing to do with all that had went on, so he would do his best to help her. "So where you trying to go because I need your ride to handle this situation. I also need to go around and find out who this Cardo cat is. I need to know just how close him and Malachi really are."

"Just take me to a hotel because I don't have anywhere else to go. I gave up everything and moved in with Dory. I just felt like I needed to be there for his recovery. You can't keep this car Daymion. It belongs to Dory and you are the last person he needs so see driving it. I'll give you the money to get one."

"You think I give a fuck about what belongs to Dory? That bitch ass mufucka ain't gave a damn about what was mine. Besides, that money you got in that envelope ain't gonna last if you coppin' rides with it. You need to be trying to hold that shit down."

Kaprice remained quiet for a few moments and then blurted out, "I've got more. A lot more."

"You have more, what?"

"I have more money. I've been stashing all the money Dory has given me, plus the money I've been pulling out of his stash. I had dreams of leaving him one day, so I can assure you that I have enough to give you some for a new ride and still have change to put you back on the map."

"The fuck you mean, put me back on the map?"

"You used to be the king of the streets. I'm just trying to help you get back on the throne. You can have every single dollar I took from him."

Daymion thought about what Kaprice was offering him but he had no intentions of going back out in the streets, and then, he thought about what kind of life he would have without them? How could he provide for him and Dre by flipping burgers for pennies?

"So, what if I take you up on your offer? What you expecting in return?"

"Just make sure I remain safe from Dory."

"I can do that, because when I get done with him, that nigga is gonna be completely useless and he ain't gonna be able to hurt you or anybody else."

"Thank you, Daymion, and for some reason, it makes me feel safer just knowing you're back in town."

Kaprice eventually gave Daymion an address. She confessed that she had rented out an apartment with some of the money she had taken from Dory. She invested in a small one bedroom on the opposite end of town just in case she ever had to dip on him and hide out. She hadn't really spent any time there because she had been too busy kissing Dory's ass. Since Daymion agreed to keep her safe, she felt like she shouldn't hold back on anything. She was glad that he understood.

"Look, we gonna go get a rental so we can ditch this ride. We'll leave it in the mall's parking garage and call a cab from there."

"That's a great idea."

Daymion pulled into one of the local malls and parked. Him and Kaprice got out and walked away from the car as quickly as they could. They walked across the street and got some food and then called a cab. The cashier was a pretty, young black girl who smiled flirtatiously at Daymion but gave Kaprice a nefarious look. Kaprice rolled her eyes at the childish act but she knew it had boosted Daymion's ego a little higher than it already was. She decided to make light of the situation and tease him about it, as soon as the girl turned around.

"Looks like you still got it Daymion, and if looks could kill, I would be lying on the floor right now."

Before he had a chance to respond to the remark, the girl was back at the counter with their order. "That will be eighteen ninety two."

Daymion looked at Kaprice and smiled, who in turn raised an eyebrow and handed him a stack of bills. She noticed the girl turn up her nose as if she just realized Daymion was a broke ass nigga. Little did she know, he was richer than she could have imagined. Daymion peeled off a fifty dollar bill and handed it to her.

"Go ahead and keep the change lil mama," and then he picked up their food before him and Kaprice walked out and got into the cab they had summoned.

On the ride to the apartment, Daymion thought about Dre while Kaprice sat back and wondered how his fresh out of prison dick would feel inside of her. It had been a long time since he had touched some pussy and she would give anything to be his first. She wanted to tell him what had happened between her and Big Gun but honestly, it wasn't his concern. She didn't want him to think that she was the type of bitch that would fuck his right hand man when times got rough. She had desired Daymion Myers for a long time and hoped that she would finally get a chance with him.

The apartment was sparsely furnished but Daymion didn't question it. However, it was as if Kaprice read his mind. "I know there's not much here but I never really had the chance to do things with it. Every time I went somewhere, Dory would give me a time limit and if I was late getting back, he would make me regret it. I was only able to get in that small sofa and table, but I do have a bed and television in the room. It's only a one bedroom but I don't mind sharing."

Daymion shook his head and chuckled at her comment. He held a lot of stress from those years in prison and true enough, he needed a release, but Kaprice wasn't the one he wanted to slide up in. "Nah, I think I'm a just chill on the couch. You know a nigga just getting out of the pen and sleeping ain't gonna be on my mind."

"Well, you know a bitch like me has the perfect stress reliever."

Kaprice walked up closer to Daymion and reached her hand down to his dick print. She knew she had him on swole so when he pulled back from her, she was confused.

"Yo, I ain't on that shit. The fuck I look like fucking you behind that bitch, Dory. It ain't gonna be that type of party so go head and dry your panties. I got shit I need to go handle so I'll holla at you later."

Kaprice was embarrassed by the rejection and hoped it didn't affect a potential relationship between them one day. Kaprice respected Daymion's gangsta so she decided to chill in hopes of one day, him making the first move. Daymion got the apartment key from her and walked out. It was time to start living his life and he decided that he would eliminate anyone who tried to stand in his way.

THUG OF SPADES 2 | COREY ROBINSON

Chapter 2

"Yo, when that nigga supposed to get out anyway? Shouldn't his time be coming to an end?" Cardo asked his friend as the two of them sat and watched game three of the NBA Finals.

"Yeah, dawg, his ass should be walking out any day now. Trust me, we gon' hear about it cause the whole block gonna be celebrating. From what I understand, he was hood famous and it's gonna be all the streets is talking about."

Dreighton sat and listened as the two men talked about his father like he wasn't in the room with them. He didn't know much about his pops and wanted to know why they hated him so much. He sat there and absorbed every single word that came out of their mouths because as soon as he could get to his father, he planned on telling him all that had been plotted against him. Dre was familiar with Cardo, but the other dude they had called Tree had just came on the scene months earlier.

"Well, whoever told you that nigga was somebody lied to your ass. That mufucka ain't no celebrity in the hood or anywhere else and I can't wait to help Malachi show him who's running shit."

About that time, Malachi walked in the living room with a half-naked Kiara trialing close behind him. Everyone went silent as is if they were afraid to speak around him. Dre looked up at the woman who had birthed him and tried to see the beauty his father had seen in her long ago, but Dre's eyes were blind to it because she had only ever showed her ugliness to him. Her heart was only cold and licentious toward him. He couldn't understand how she worshipped the ground Malachi walked on even after he treated her like shit on the bottom of his Timbs. Dre had grown tired of trying to please her because it seemed that nothing he did was good enough. The only time she showed him attention was when his pockets were laced. He would come in from the block and hand Cardo his cut and before he could slide the rest back in his pocket, Kiara snatched it away. Dre finally grew tired of his hard earned dollars being taken so he dug a small hole behind an abandoned house and buried his money in a box.

"The fuck you niggas stop talking for? Make me feel like y'all bitches sitting up in here plotting on my ass. Sup with that?" Malachi inquired as he sat down and pulled Kiara onto his lap. He looked at Dre and scoffed and then pinched one of Kiara's hardened nipples. Dre had gotten used to the disrespect that Malachi showed him but it just didn't faze him anymore.

Cardo laughed at the question and pulled out a spliff, but before he lit it, he responded. "Damn Mal, you too fuckin' paranoid, bruh. Don't you know I'd slit my own throat before I'd plot against you?"

Cardo lit the blunt and passed it to Tree who took a pull and stated. "We was just talking about that nigga, Day. Mufucka should be walking out of those gates any day now. We ready to show him who's running thangs these days."

"Yeah. The nigga betta know his place or he can get dealt with. Just make sure you stay in good with him until we can find out the moves he's gonna make," Malachi stated and pulled Kiara in for a long tongue kiss, while he kneaded her breast.

Tree shook his head and spoke up. "Nigga, you foul as fuck. I'ma get outta here and take Dre with me. There's money out there to be made and sitting up in this bitch ain't filling my pockets. I damn sure ain't about to miss it. Lets jet, Lil Spade."

Dre had got the name Spade from Teddy and at first, he hated it, but as time passed on and him and Teddy became closer he began to embrace it. He also felt like he was honoring Teddy by using it. Dre wasn't familiar with Tree but he jumped up quickly and headed for the door. Any opportunity he had to get away from Malachi was one he took. Plus, he didn't want to sit there and continue to watch his mother get treated like a whore.

He could hear Malachi talk shit in the background as he walked out. "Yeah, get that mufucka outta here so he can go make me some money. I'm tired of his ass sitting there watching me like he want to be on my dick instead of his momma."

Dre shook his head and got into Tree's ride while murderous thoughts filled his mind. "One day, I'm a kill that mufucka."

"That's some big words for a small time nigga like you. May want to build up your muscle before you go fucking with Malachi. Especially if you tryin' to take him out like that."

"Fuck Malachi. He gon' get his. Mark my words."

Dre had thought about killing Malachi many times but had yet to figure out how he would pull it off. Unlike Kiara, he wanted to escape the hold Malachi had on him. He just couldn't fathom how Kiara could continue letting his bitch ass treat her that way. Dre had given up on trying to save her, so he decided he would focus on saving himself instead. Tree's words broke him from his thoughts.

"How you feel about making some extra cash? I got some shit that will triple what you making right now."

Dre wasn't sure if he was being serious or not, plus, he didn't know if he could trust him. It could have been a trick to see if he would go behind Malachi's back. The only thing Dre could think to do was turn him down.

"Nah, I think I can manage. Why you ask me that anyway? Cardo and Malachi know you going behind they back or did they put you up to it?"

"Them mufuckas ain't gotta know everything. Besides, I know you trying to get out from under them. You could make enough loot to dip on they greedy asses and they won't even see it coming. Shit, you gon' be making so much, the bitches gonna be dropping they panties on sight. You might still be young but I know that dick gets hard."

Tree laughed at his own joke but Dre didn't find shit funny. "Why you trying to help me out? You don't even know me like that."

"I do know you like that. I fucks with your pops. I was locked up with him for three years and you were all he talked about."

"Nigga, you 'ont know my daddy, besides, I heard you and Cardo talk that shit about him."

"It ain't even like that. I'm only rolling with them mufuckas to find out what they plan is. I know about the old beef between Malachi and your pops, but your pops don't know about it. He thinks that his only enemy is Dory so he ain't gon' see Malachi coming his way."

Dre turned his head and looked at Tree to see if he could pick up on his vibe, but he couldn't read him. "How I know you ain't lying? Why you ain't never said nothing to me about it before and why you let that nigga treat my momma that way?"

"Why the hell you care how he treats her? She don't give a fuck about you. Besides, she obviously likes that shit or she'd leave his ass alone. Some women like it when a nigga dogs them out. And I ain't mention your pops because I gotta stay in character with them mufuckas. If you would have known that I was cool with Daymion, your ass would have started asking questions. You woulda got comfortable and they would have picked up on that shit. My black ass ain't trying to get murked around this bitch. Shit, right now, I gotta play along."

"And why should I believe you? If you playing them, how I know you ain't playing me too?"

"You a smart mufucka but, the question is, why shouldn't you believe me? It ain't like you got shit else to believe in. I mean, look at ya momma and that shit she let them niggas do in front of you. Ya pops locked the fuck up and you basically out here on ya own. You gotta believe in something. Might as well be me."

Dre got quiet and thought about what he had said. He did want to make some extra cash because once he got enough money saved up he planned on dipping but he still wasn't sure if the man was trying to set him up or not. "What you got that you trying to get rid of?"

"Lil nigga I got that boy and that shit gonna put mufuckas on they toes. That stuff Cardo and Mal got you out there with is only teasing them fiends. It done played out. Them crackheads want something stronger. Something that's gonna make them feel even better and we gon' give 'em just what they asking for. So, what do you say? You down with me or not?"

Dre didn't know what Boy was but since he wasn't a fiend and wouldn't be doing it he decided that it really didn't matter. If that's what they wanted then that's what they would get. He was good and ready to get out of Cardo and Mal's grasp. If his momma wanted to stay then that shit was on her but he was ready to be his own man. Fuck everyone else.

"So, when you want to get me started on it?"

"Lil nigga, I can stack you up right now. See, that's the shit I like about you right there. Your lil ass stay ready and a nigga like me can't do nothing but respect that."

Tree turned down a side street and stopped. When he pulled up the floor board and revealed a secret compartment, Dre's eyes grew big. He watched Tree pull out a black silk bag and hoped that the product was all that he had promised. Dre could already see the dollar signs in his vision but he wasn't greedy. He planned on sharing with Kenny and Tasha. They were his best and only friends and all of them ate together. This time would be no different. Tree pulled out ten baggies and passed them to Dre and explained how shit went. Dre grasped the baggies tightly before shoving them into the pocket of his jeans, and then asked, "You sho' this is what them fiends want?"

"Lil nigga, I ain't neva been more sure of anything in my life. Them little pockets you got on them jeans 'bout to burst at the seams. That shit I just gave you is gonna put your lil ass on the map and each time you come to re-up I'm a give you more and more. Shit, one day you could be the king of the streets. Your pops is gonna be real proud. Now, get on out there and bring in that bacon."

Dre pulled on his skully and jacket and then stepped out in the cool night breeze looking like the young thug that he was. He stood and waited for Tree to pull off before he cut through the woods. There was no way he could see himself put new product out in the streets without his right hands, Kenny and Tasha. They hadn't been out as much since Tasha killed Malice for raping her but Dre hoped that if he showed up and propositioned them, they would have his back.

By the time Dre had made it to his best friend's grandmother's house, his hands were frozen and it caused his knuckles to sting when he knocked on the wooden door.

All the lights were on so he knew that they were home. He just wished that someone would hurry up and open the door so he could get warm. He blew into his palms and felt a sense of relief when he heard the locks release and Kenny's face appear.

"Sup Dre, we was about to sit down and eat but you can come in and join us. You know grandma ain't gonna mind. Besides, she always makes enough to feed an army."

"Yeah man, I'm hungry as hell but I need to talk to you about something first."

"Ah come on, my black ass is hungry. Can't we talk after we eat?"

Dre didn't want to wait but he had to admit that he could use a hot meal. He had grown accustomed to eating cold leftovers that sat in the refrigerator at Malachi's. He decided to put off what he needed to say until after they ate like Kenny asked. "Alright, but the shit I need to run by you is serious."

"Alright. Alright. As soon as we eat. I promise."

Dre took off his jacket and followed Kenny into the dining room where Tasha and their grandmother, Miss Dot sat. Dre knew that he had always been welcome there but for some reason he felt a little nervous. Perhaps, because of the ten packs of heroin in his pocket. Miss Dot looked up at Dre and smiled but to him it felt like she knew what he was holding. It was like she could read him.

"It looks like you get skinnier every time I see you but if you keep showing up over here, I'm a fatten you up. Sit on down and fix you a plate. There's plenty for everyone."

She watched Dre sit down and lick his lips. She didn't know everything that had been going on in his life but she knew that he was Kiara Taylors boy and was sure that he wasn't being cared for. She had never been one to pry in other people's business but she could tell that Dre was a good kid and she had a mind to go over to Kiara's and tell her how she felt. The only thing that stopped her was Kiara's man, Malachi Jensen. Miss Dot knew that he was bad news and couldn't afford to bring drama to her front door. She had Kenny and Tasha to take care of and needed to protect them at all costs. When she noticed Dre eating his food at a rapid pace, she had to say something.

"Young man. Don't you think you should slow down? You're gonna make yourself sick."

Dre felt embarrassed by her comment and put his fork down. "Sorry, Miss Dot. I guess I was hungrier than I thought. I'm full now, so can I be excused? I got things I need to go do."

Miss Dot nodded her head and gave him permission to leave the table. She wondered what things someone so young had to do and hoped it didn't involve anything criminal. When Dre got up, Tasha and Kenny followed suit and the three of them walked out together on the front porch.

"Hey, I got a hold of some new shit for us to put out there to them fiends. I'm told it's more potent than what Cardo been giving us and our pockets are gonna fill up faster. Ya'll down with me?"

Tasha smiled and batted her long eyelashes at Dre. He had known for a while that she had a thing for him but he would never entertain it because his heart belonged to Shay, and once he fattened up his pockets, he would search for her. She had disappeared after she shot Dory and hadn't reached back out to Dre. He had been shattered ever since. However, he knew that Tasha would be down for whatever he asked as long as she could roll with him.

"Hell yeah. You know I'm always down for whatever you bring. Count me all the way in."

Kenny looked at his sister and shook his head because he too knew how she felt about their friend. He tried to tell her on several occasions that she didn't stand a chance but Tasha was hard headed and refused to listen. He knew that one day she would regret it. "Nah Dre. I don't think that's a good idea. What you think Cardo gonna do if he finds out we on the block selling shit for someone else? Man, his crazy ass gon' kill us."

"Fuck Cardo and fuck Malachi's ass too. Them greedy motherfuckers don't wanna see us come up but I refuse to let them keep a hold on me so I'm going to make this money with or without y'all."

Kenny hated to let his friend down but he knew the consequences of going behind Cardo's back especially with product from someone else. "Aye Dre. you don't think that shit's a little shady since the nigga that gave it to you is supposed to be cool with Cardo? You don't feel like that shit's a set up?"

"Yo, you down or what? That's all I need to know right now. I'll deal with the rest of that shit later."

Kenny held up his hands and gave Dre the answer he didn't want to hear. "Sorry Dre, but I'm a have to pass on this one. Shit just don't feel right to me. Come on Tasha, let's go back inside."

Tasha hesitated because the last thing she wanted to do was let Dre down but she also knew that if she went without Kenny, there would be hell to pay when she got home. "Sorry Dre, but please be careful out there."

After his friends went back inside, Dre stood alone on the porch for a minute, stunned. He couldn't believe that they didn't want to go along with him. He really thought that he could depend on them but now he questioned their friendship. He looked back at the door with a scowl on his face and shook his head. He wasn't mad at them, just hurt because he thought that no matter what, they would stick by him. He didn't have time to stand there and worry about it though. There was money to be made and he'd be damned if he let their decisions stop him from getting it. So, Dre zipped up his jacket and pulled up the hoodie over the skully he already wore. He was a Myers and one day he would rule the hood and be somebody that they could look up to, just like his father.

THUG OF SPADES 2 | COREY ROBINSON

When Dre cut back through the path to get to his corner, the fiends were already waiting. "Aye Dre, let me get a fifty piece of that fire. You know you got the best shit around here."

The crackhead that towered over him was a loyal customer and always seeked Dre out before anybody else. He decided to try the new product on the fiend and hoped he would spread the word.

Dre looked up into the blood shot eyes of the fiend and did his sales pitch. He knew he had to start off with someone and the fiend before him was perfect. "Hey, I got some new shit but I need someone to test it and put the word out. You game?"

The fiend smiled at the thought of getting a free high and quickly agreed. "Hell yeah I'm game. What you got for me?"

When Dre pulled out one of the packs of dope, the fiend backed up and shook his head. Dre didn't understand why the package spooked the man. "Aye, what's up man? Why you backing up like you scared or something? Shit is just some heroin and it's gonna make you feel better than that crack shit."

When the man pointed behind Dre, he slowly turned around to see what the dude was looking at and when he did, he almost pissed himself. Malachi lifted Dre by the hoodie on his jacket so that they were eye to eye. "You little mufucka. You out here trying to sell another man's shit on my fucking block? The fuck you think you are? Huh? You little bitch? Who the hell gave you that shit and you better not lie."

Dre stared Malachi in the eyes but didn't open his mouth. He may have only been seventeen but he knew the code of the streets so he wasn't about to tell Malachi shit. He knew that he would suffer for it later but a few bumps and bruises were nothing compared to being labeled a snitch. When

Malachi realized that Dre wasn't going to answer him, he dropped him on the ground and spit on him after he landed on his ass.

"Get you fuck ass up and get in my car. I'm a teach you about being disloyal to me and my crew, nigga. You make money for my set and ain't no one gonna get in the way of that. Now let's go."

Young Dre got up and dusted off the back of his jeans. He looked up the block and thought about running but knew that he wouldn't make it very far. His ass hurt from landing on it but he refused to let Malachi see him in pain. He wished that he would have followed Kenny's advice but it was too late to turn back. He jumped when Malachi started the car and then walked slowly toward it. He knew that he was in for a long night and mentally prepared himself on the ride home.

Malachi said nothing the entire ride and the tension could be cut with a knife. Dre wondered who had sold him out and hoped that it wasn't his best friend because that would have changed everything. When they finally pulled up in the yard, Dre went to open his door but before he could get a hand on the latch, he was snatched across the seat and through the driver side door, "Think your ass gonna get away with that shit? I'm a beat your ass til you tell me what the fuck I wanna know."

Cardo, Tree and Kiara sat in the living room sharing a joint when Malachi drug Dre through the front door. Neither of them got up to help him, but instead watched as the man of the house beat him with a belt after ripping off his jacket and T-shirt. The welts rose quickly on Dre's dark skin and eventually he became numb to the blows. After Malachi's arm grew tired, he finally stopped and left him lying on the ground, his skin bruised and bloody.

Dre could hear his mother's voice even through the ringing in his ears and it made his hate for her deepen. "What did the bastard do now?"

"That mufucka thought he was gonna sell someone else's dope on my block and get away with it. I don't know who the fuck told him that was okay but I had to show his ass that I run shit around here and next time I won't be so fucking easy on him."

Dre lifted his head and looked up into Tree's eyes. Tree nodded his head at him and Dre wasn't sure what the nod meant but he took it as a thanks for not selling him out. The thought never crossed his mind that Tree had sent Malachi out to the block to check on him because he seemed like the type of nigga who didn't want his money compromised. Dre was in so much pain he could barely move but somehow he found the strength to get up and go into the small bedroom that he slept in. When he shut the door, that is when the first tear drop fell from his saddened eyes. He would get it all out that night because he vowed it would be the last tears that blinded him. From that night on, he would plan his payback. He didn't know how and he didn't know when but he would give Malachi a dose of his own medicine. With those thoughts in mind, Dre closed his eyes and fell asleep.

Chapter 3

Daymion took his time and looked around before he crept up into the yard. He pulled the key that he had been given out of his pocket and held it tightly between his fingers. He didn't mask up because he wanted the man inside the house to see his face. He wanted the man to look him in the eyes so he would know without a doubt that he wasn't there to play games. The encounter would be a long time coming because the beef between them was an old one that had never been squashed.

The wooden planks creaked when Day stepped up on the porch but he refused to let that be a setback and when he slid the silver key into the lock and turned, the door opened with ease. The house was pitch black but Day didn't need any light because he was familiar with the entire layout. The place had once been a trap house that his soldiers made money out of and he could walk room to room blindfolded if he had to. He could smell the sweet scent of a woman as it lingered in the air and if he didn't know any better he would have sworn that she was standing next to him.

Day was half way through the living room when he felt a presence and stopped. He wasn't caught off guard because he had expected as much. When the light came on, Day stared down at the man in the wheelchair and shook his head. Dory sat wide eyed and stared back at him while he held a black Ruger .380 in his hand. Daymion knew that he wouldn't really pull the trigger because Dory had always been a pussy and Day could see the slight tremble in his fingers.

"The fuck you doing in my shit? Don't you know better than to come up in places you don't belong?"

Day let out a small chuckle because the nigga in front of him tried to appear tough, a side of the man that he could respect if things would have been different. "Last time I checked, this here was my shit and me being gone all this time ain't changed that. I would kick your ass up outta here but from the looks of things, your crippled ass wouldn't get very far."

"Man, fuck you. This wheelchair ain't stopping shit! My legs may not be in top gear but ain't a damn thing wrong with my trigger finger so I'm a give you thirty seconds to turn around and go back out the same way you came in."

"Nah, I ain't going nowhere until I get what the fuck I came for but if you feeling bold, go ahead and bust a cap my nigga."

"Ain't shit here for you so I don't know what the fuck you talking about."

"You know exactly what I'm talking about so stop playing dumb, mufucka."

Before Dory could get out another word, Day pulled a metal bat out from behind his back and swung. The gun flew from Dory's hand and landed behind the couch with a thud. He looked up at Day and quickly gripped the wheels of his chair but Day pushed the handle of the bat through a space in the wheel frame and put Dory's idea of getting away on hold.

"You ain't going nowhere mufucka until I get some answers."

"Come on, Day. The fuck you want from me man? You came up in here unannounced and thought that I was just gonna let you run up on me without pulling out my piece?"

35

Daymion towered over Dory and thought about his options. While he did that time up the road, he had made a vow to himself that he would change and do things differently once he got out but the streets was in his blood and deep down he knew there wasn't shit he could do about it.

"Yo mane, my bitch will probably be home soon so you may want to leave before she gets here. Hell, her ass might freak the fuck out and call them crackas and I'm willing to bet a stack that the police are the last people you want to run into. I think it's best we keep this shit between us. No hard feelings."

Daymion scoffed at his comment because he knew that no one was going to show up there. "Don't worry about your bitch. She ain't coming back."

"The fuck you talking about, Day? What the hell you do to her?"

"I gave her this muthafuckin dick nigga and now she stuck. You ain't gotta never worry about her again. But I ain't here to discuss a bitch. I'm here to talk about my son."

"Your son? I 'ont know shit about that lil mufucka so you wasting your time."

Daymion lifted the bat and brought it down on Dory's right shoulder.

"Aah, shit. Okay, okay. You ain't gotta do all that Day."

"Then, tell me where the fuck my son is at and explain to me why you had him out there working the block."

"Aye, that lil nigga came to me about putting him on. Said he wanted to help his momma out with some of the bills. I did the kid a favor so you should be here thanking me for giving his ass a chance."

"Thanking you? Bitch, you don't deserve any thanks for me. You sent my son out there and then turned around and sent your lil brother out to try and rob him just so you could put him in debt to you as a payback to that bullshit beef we had going on. Nigga, that shit was between us and my seed ain't got a damn thing to do with it."

"Now come on, Day, you know it's rough out there on them blocks. Malice was just trying to toughen his soft ass up."

Daymion swung the bat again and made contact with Dory's right knee.

"Aah fuck, come on my nigga. I'm just learning how to walk again."

"Oh really? Well, if you keep fucking around, I'ma make it to where you forget any steps you've ever made. Stop testing my patience and tell me where to find my son."

Dory stared at Daymion but said nothing until Daymion lifted the bat again.

"Wait, wait, wait. Damn. I can tell you who he's with but I can't tell you where that nigga stay at. Just don't hit me with the bat again."

Daymion pulled up a chair and sat in front of Dory. His nose flared as he waited for an answer but before Dory could speak, a voice came from behind.

"I know where he's at, but you gotta take me with you."

Daymion jumped out of the chair and turned around. He had never seen the young woman before but she didn't seem like a threat. He didn't see any weapons but still remained cautious. "Who the hell are you?"

The woman walked up close to him and studied his face. She stared and then reached a hand up to touch him but Daymion backed up because he had no clue what was going on. "My God, he looks just like you."

"Who the hell are you? I won't ask again."

Dory spoke from behind. "That's the little bitch that put this slug in my back and took all my money. Go head, Day and kill that bitch. She don't have no info for you. She's just playin' your ass."

The young woman laughed and reached for Daymion's bat. He let it go and she took it with ease and swung. When the bat made contact with Dory's other knee, Daymion heard bones crack.

"Aah, aah. Bitch, I'm a kill your ass."

"Oh yeah? Didn't you try that before? Looks like you're not very good at it."

She turned back to Daymion while Dory struggled with the pain he was in. She had spared him the first time but she would show him no more mercy.

"My name is Monshay. Your son and I are very close but I haven't had any contact with him in a while. However, I have been keeping tabs on him."

"The fuck you mean close? How close?"

Before Shay could answer the question, Dory spoke up. "Ya boy got a thang for her but he got to get his status up to fuck with a bitch like her. Dick too small right now."

Shay ignored his comment because she had always known that Dory envied Dre, and she could understand why. Dre was only seventeen but he was still more man than Dory could ever be. Daymion wanted to know if what Dory spoke was true, so he asked.

"What that nigga talking about? What's up with you and my boy? Something going on between y'all? How old are you anyway?"

"I'm about to turn nineteen and yes. Dre and I have a strong attraction to each other. He means the world to me but we ain't serious yet."

Daymion could tell from the look in her eyes that whatever Shay was feeling was real, and he couldn't fault his son for being attracted to her because she truly was a beauty. Even the small scar that adorned her right cheek gave her definition. It seemed to add a sense of reality to her opulent demeanor. She seemed familiar to him but he brushed the feeling away as he looked deep into her amber colored eyes and asked what he wanted to know.

"How the hell you end up with this nigga? Ain't you a little young for his sorry ass?"

Shay glanced at Dory who sat quietly with a devious look in his eyes. She knew him very well and as soon as he saw an opportunity, he would make a move but she was not going to allow it. She pulled some zip ties out of her bag and walked over to him.

"The fuck you gonna do with those?"

"Oh Dory. I know you so well and I'm just gonna make sure you stay put because whatever you're sitting there plotting ain't gonna happen."

Dory put his hands on the wheels of the chair in hopes to make a dash. He wished that he had listened to Kaprice when she told him to invest in an electric wheelchair but Dory never guessed he would be in one for as long as he had. As soon as he wrapped his fingers around the edges of the wheels, Daymion reached down and grabbed his wrists.

"Going somewhere playa?"

Dory looked from Daymion to Shay and knew that he was fucked. "How the hell y'all gon' come up in my shit and do this to me? What y'all looking for ain't here so go the fuck on."

While Shay put the ties around Dory's wrists and attached them to the wheels, she responded to Daymion's question. "I met Dory through Teddy, my brother. I was seventeen when I met him and he treated me like a queen. I thought he was the most winsome and indomitable man I'd ever met, but come to find out, he was just an impostor. By the time, he showed his true colors, I was stuck."

"So, how is my son a part of all this? And if Dre means so much to you, why the hell haven't you went for him?"

"Dre showed up here one day and asked Dory for some work. Dory only gave it to him because he knew Dre was your son. He had bad intentions from the start. I took to him instantly along with Teddy and when we found out Malice was trying to rob him, we decided to pay Dory with his own money. I started taking from his stash and giving it to Dre. Dory finally caught me and put a stop to it. Dre ran off for some reason and now, he's in Cardo and Malachi's clutches, along with his mother."

Daymion turned his head to look back at Dory who had surprisingly remained quiet, and then, he turned back to Shay. "I'm a need you to come with me. You gon' take me to those niggas."

"And what about Dory?"

"Fuck that nigga. Leave his ass just like that. As long as his hands is tied to them wheels, he ain't going nowhere. We can deal with him later."

Dory heard the words that slid off Day's tongue and finally spoke up. "Aye bruh, you can't leave a nigga like this. How the hell am I supposed to piss and do other shit? I told you I'd keep this between us. Just leave me out of that bullshit you about to start with Jensen. I ain't gonna talk."

Daymion and Shay looked at each other but neither of them felt any concern for Dory. He had made his bed and now he had to lie in it. Shay looked at him and couldn't believe that she had actually felt for him at one time. However, she would not make that same mistake again. She thought about all the things he had put her through and wanted her payback. She wanted to give him everything he deserved.

Day finally broke her out of the trance she was in. "Come on. Let's get out of here. We can deal with his ass later because he's the least of our worries right now."

"Yo, y'all muthafuckas can't leave me like this. Cut this shit off my wrists. I ain't going nowhere. Come on, look at me. I can't even fucking walk."

Dory continued to beg but neither Day nor Shay had any sympathy for him. Dory was a heartless bastard who deserved nothing less than what he would ultimately get.

"Let's go Shay. Just leave that nigga."

"Nah, I need to close his mouth. If he keeps hollering like a bitch someone is bound to hear him and I don't want them to have the opportunity to save him from what I got planned. I owe his black ass for a lot of bullshit he did so I gotta make sure he's where I need him to be."

"Aight but look, I'm a be in my car waiting. I'll give you a few minutes to handle your business but be quick. I mean, I know the nigga got a big mouth but don't let it take you all night."

"Okay. I won't take too long."

As soon as Day walked out of the house, Shay picked up the baseball bat that he had left behind. Dory looked at Shay through wide eyes and although he already knew what was about to go down he asked her anyway.

"What the hell you about to do, Shay? Huh? Why you still living in the past? Go on and follow that nigga out so y'all can go find that lil mufucka you betrayed me for."

"Ya know Dory. I never would have stabbed you in the back if you wouldn't have stabbed me first. You gave me my first broken heart long before I did anything to you."

"The fuck is you talking about? I beat your ass because you was robbing me and giving my money to that lil bastard to pay me with and I ain't fuck with Teddy until you pulled that shit. I couldn't let you get away with that."

"I'm not talking about what you did to me or even what you did to Teddy. I'm talking about what you did to my mother."

"Your mother? Bitch what the fuck is you talking about? Who the hell is your damn mother?"

"Malia was my momma and it's because of you she's dead. It's your fault she got shot that night."

Dory could not believe what he had just heard. She had to be lying because Malia had never mentioned having a

41

daughter. He remembered how overjoyed she was about the baby she had been carrying when she was killed but she never said she'd had one before.

"Bitch, get out of her with that bullshit. There's no way Malia was your momma and if she was, how come she never mentioned your ass?"

"She was only thirteen when she had me and knew that she couldn't take care of me so she sent me to live with my uncle. Those times she would be gone from you, she would be with me. Teddy was my uncle's son but because I grew up with him, he was more like my brother than a cousin. The two people I loved most in this world are gone because of you."

"Look, I didn't kill Malia. She was hit by a stray bullet that the nigga you about to ride off with shot from his gun. So you take that shit up with his ass and leave me out of it. I loved her and I never would have brought her any harm. Don't blame that on me."

Before Dory finished his sentence good, the bat came down on his shin.

"Aah shit. What the fuck did you do that for?"

"You didn't love my mother. You just didn't want my father to have her. She was scared to leave because you threatened the baby she was carrying. A baby that you tried to make people think was yours but we all know that it wasn't and the only reason my mother was hit with that bullet was because you pulled her in front of you so it would hit her instead of you."

"What? See, now you sound crazy as hell. Why would I want to harm her?"

"Because you would have rather her be dead than to be with my father and you knew that it was his child she was carrying. Now you got to pay for that shit. That bullet might have missed you but I can assure you, mine won't." Dory sat there stunned at all Shay had just told him. He had laid with the woman in front of him and never saw the resemblance to

Malia until then. How could he have missed it? He had slept with the enemy's woman for so long and to find out that he could have been sleeping with the enemy's daughter too had him feeling disgruntled.

"Hold up. What the fuck are you saying? Who the hell is your father?"

Shay smiled deviously before she responded to his question. "My father is Malachi Jensen and don't worry Dory, he will get his too."

Shay pulled out the gun that she'd had concealed behind her back and aimed it at Dory. His eyes grew big as he begged for his life. "Come on, Shay. Shit ain't got to come to this. We can work all this out and be the way that we used to be. Remember those days? Huh? You know a nigga made you happy but you fucked us up. You caused this rift between us. I'm sorry about Malia. I, I, I wasn't even thinking when I pulled her in front of me but I did love her. I did, and I loved you too. I still love you. Let's just work this out."

"There's nothing for us to work out. What's done is done and because of you, I had to grow up without her. She was my world Dory, my world. I needed her and because of you, I don't have her. All those nights I spent lying beside you I was plotting for when this day came and now that it's here, I'm going to give you just what you deserve."

Shay pulled the trigger on the small gun she held and watched as the blood spewed out. The impact took Dory's breath away and when he looked up into her eyes she felt chills covering her body. She turned to leave but thought about it and turned back to face him. "I'll see you when I get to hell, Dory."

Shay walked away and felt like she could still hear the curdling sounds that came from Dory's throat. She figured that his lungs should be filled with blood by the time she got to the last step that led her away from the porch. When

Daymion saw her come out, he rolled down his window and started his ride.

"You good now?"

"Yeah, I'm good but I ain't done yet." She smiled and got in her car so she could follow Day. She wasn't sure how he was going to react when he found out that she was Malachi and Malia's daughter. For a long time, she had hated Day because the slug came from a gun he had aimed but when she found out that it was aimed at Dory and not Malia, she found a way to cope and to understand. She finally forgave him.

When Day pulled into the apartment complex, Shay pulled in beside him and parked. She wondered how he had found the place because she had lived in the city all of her life and had never heard of it. She was lost in thought when a sudden knock on her window startled her, so she shut her engine off and got out.

"Aye, you aight? You ain't feeling bad about what you did back there are you?"

"Bad? Hell no. I've never felt better about anything. It's such a relief to have that chapter of my life over with. I've waited so long to do that."

Daymion looked at her sideways and wondered if there was more to her story but he would save that question for another day. "Come on up. We got a lot of shit to work out. I'm a call up my boy, Branch and see if he has any information that could help us."

"Help us how? I know where Malachi rests his head. All we gotta do is run up in there and handle him the same way we did Dory."

"Oh yeah? You acting like you know a lot about that nigga but regardless, we ain't running up in nothing. My son is allegedly there and I don't want to put him in danger. I did time with Branch and I know he's gonna have my back. He don't know I'm home yet but I know he'll come if I call."

"Okay, I'll do whatever you say. I just want to get to Dre."

Shay followed Daymion's footsteps until they got to the door of an apartment in the last building on the lot. She wondered why he had parked so far away from the place. "Why didn't you just park in front of this building and save us a trip?"

"Nah, I don't know if someone could have followed us so things are better and safer this way. If there would have been someone behind us, by the time we got to the door, I would have noticed them. Anything I do that seems strange to you is merely a habit for me. You in good hands so just chill."

Shay listened and raised her eyebrows. She had no other choice but to trust him if she wanted to see Dre again. She walked behind him into the apartment and heard a woman's voice, a very familiar one.

"Oh my God, Daymion. I have been so worried. I'm so glad you're alright. How did things go with Dory? Did he say anything about me?"

Kaprice rambled on not knowing that Day had brought some company.

"I'm good but I can't say the same for that nigga, but I think I have a lead on finding what I'm looking for."

He finally moved to the side and that was when the two women saw each other. Kaprice was the first to speak up. "Oh, hell no. How did you run into this bitch and why is she here?"

"Oh uh uh, I ain't staying up in here with her ass. How could you possibly be involved with her?"

"Come on now ladies, we are all adults here so whatever bullshit y'all got going on here has got to be left behind. This shit is about my son and nothing else should matter so put those fucking attitudes in check."

Shay gave Kaprice a look of disgust but knew that it would be better for her in the end if she respected Daymion's wishes. The last thing she wanted to do was piss him off. She had to look past the fact that Kaprice had been fucking Dory the day that her and Dre had walked in and robbed him. As bad as she wanted to curse Kaprice out, she would hold her words and save them for another day. She would make sure to keep a close eye on her though, because her gut told her that she couldn't be trusted.

"Look Daymion, you know I don't mind chilling and helping you out however I can but what the hell does this bitch need to be here for? This bitch brought your son to Dory's to help her rob him. What if that bullet would have hit your son instead of Dory? She's a fucking liability if you ask me."

"Yeah? Well, ain't nobody asked you shit so let me worry about her. For now, you two need to try and get along."

Daymion walked out of the living room and left the two of them standing there. They could fight or do whatever they needed to do but they better learn how to tolerate each other. He needed to clear his head so he could make that call to Branch. He was anxious to hook back up with his old cellmate because deep down, he felt like Branch was the only one he could trust.

He also wanted to reach out to Kayla, not only because sliding up in some warm, wet pussy would be nice, but because he genuinely missed her. He decided to handle his little issue, get Dre and go to the woman he hoped he could spend forever with.

Chapter 4

Dre felt the presence above him as he lied on the soiled mattress that had been set up for him on the floor. It wasn't the best but it was comfortable and gave him a place to rest his head. He wasn't sure if he wanted to open his eyes and turn over to face whoever it was that looked down upon him but he also couldn't just continue to lie there and pretend to be asleep. He could still feel the hot pain as it seared through his body and reminded him of the night before. He had cried his last tears and swore that it would be the last time he allowed Malachi to put his hands on him. Dre finally opened his eyes and turned to see who it was that stalked him.

"Get up. I got some shit I wanna talk to you about."

Tree's six foot statue hovered above him like a giant statue and as Dre tried to sit up, the pain knocked him back down. He tried not to show any weakness to the man so he sat back up as quickly as he'd went down.

"Where's Malachi and Cardo?"

"Don't worry about them. They gone on a run but they'll be back soon. I wanted to holla at you while they out so get up and get yourself right."

"Nah, I'm good. You got me in enough shit so I think I'll pass."

"Lil nigga I ain't ask you what you wanted. Now get your ass in gear.

Dre finally stood up from the mattress and looked at Tree through tired eyes wondering what he had to say. He felt like the man had put him in a bad position by going against Malachi but he also knew that the damage had been done. His betrayal would not be forgotten and would be held against him for the rest of his life however, he wasn't trying to dig his hole any deeper.

"I need a minute to go take care of my hygiene unless you'd rather talk to me like this."

"Ya know what? You a sarcastic lil nigga but I'm a let you handle that breath. Make that shit quick though. They'll be back soon."

Tree turned and walked out of the small room, while Dre stood and thought about his options which were very few. He wished that he could run away and hide but he had no clue where to go. He didn't quite know when his father was coming home but hoped that it was soon so he could take him away from everything, especially his mother. He wasn't a child anymore, but he had nowhere else to turn.

Dre stepped into the bathroom and closed the door behind him. He looked into the mirror and then up at the small window that was slightly ajar. He thought about taking a chance and climbing out of it but he had no clue where he would go from there. He thought about Kenny and Tasha. He couldn't believe that they had turned him down. He had thought that they would ride with him no matter what but boy, was he wrong. He was only trying to make them all come up in the game together but realized that Kenny was a pussy. He knew that if he got Tasha alone, she would ride. He was aware of how she felt about him and even though she would never own a piece of his heart, she would be beneficial to his future.

The sudden banging on the door broke Dre from his thoughts. "Man, what the hell is taking you so long? Bring your ass out here. We ain't got all day."

Dre looked at the small window once again and pursed his lips together. He was too young to deal with so much but until his father came home, he had to make the best of it. He opened the door slowly and looked up at Tree with an attitude. "I'm coming. I just needed a second."

"Yeah. I feel like you was thinking about dipping on me through that window in there but I'm glad you smarter than that. Come on."

Dre followed him into the kitchen and noticed a plate of food on the table. His stomach instantly growled and caused Tree to laugh. "Man, sit your hungry ass down and eat. I can't let you be out on them block with my shit and be all hungry. I need you to focus on what's important when you out there."

"I can't go back out there for you, man. Malachi gonna end up killing me for that."

Tree pulled out the chair and motioned for Dre to sit down. He knew that he was probably starving because all Kiara fed him was leftovers and the portions wouldn't even fill up a three year old. In a way, Tree felt bad for the kid but when it came to his money, that shit went out the window.

"Oh, you going back out there and you ain't got to worry about Mal. If his ass come for you, pull this out on him and he'll back the fuck up."

Tree pulled out a small pistol and sat it on the table beside Dre's plate. The sound of the metal landing on the table caused Dre to jump. His eyes grew wide because he wasn't sure what the gun meant. He didn't know if he should feel threatened or not so he just sat there and hoped that he could get an answer.

"What's the matter kid? You scared of this piece of metal here? Huh? Shit, you Daymion Myers son. You ain't 'pose to be scared of a damn thing."

"I ain't scared. I'm just trying to figure out what you doing with it. Why you sat it by my food?"

"Ya know, you real damn funny. This is for you."

"What you want me to do with it?"

"Come on kid. You hold this thing out in front of you and you'll never have to worry about Malachi putting his hands on you again. That nigga gonna back the fuck up away from you as long as you got this." He picked the gun up and pointed it at Dre. "This right here gives you all the power you need. You can do shit your way. Come on and hold it in your hand. Get that feeling of being a boss.

Dre hesitated because he wasn't exactly sure of what to do but when he heard the locks on the front door, he quickly grabbed it and put it down the waist of his jeans. No sooner than he'd pulled his shirt over it, Malachi and Cardo walked in.

"The fuck is going on up in here?"

"Ain't shit dawg. Just letting the kid have the rest of my breakfast. I could hear his stomach growling from the next room. Mufucka hungry as hell."

Malachi picked up the plate of food just as Kiara walked in with her arms full of bags of groceries. He looked at her and winked before he turned back to Dre. "Yeah, well his hungry ass gotta earn his keep and as far as I can tell he ain't earned a damn thing. Get your ugly ass up and go make some money and then we can talk about filling your stomach when you get back."

Kiara let out a light chuckle while she put the groceries away. Dre looked at her and wondered if she would ever treat him like a real son. He held so much anger and hurt inside his heart, he felt like it would burst in his chest.

He backed away when Malachi walked up on him closer, "Don't let me catch you out there selling shit you ain't get from me. You already know what's going to happen if you do. So, are we clear on that?"

Dre just stood there and didn't answer him right away so Malachi slapped him upside the head. "Are we clear? Huh?"

"Yeah, you clear. You ain't gotta worry."

"Aight, that's good to know. Now get the hell outta here and handle my business. Us grown folks got stuff we need to do."

Dre looked around the room at all the eyes that looked back at him and swore to himself that one day, he would shut them for good. He had no choice but to play their little game for now but he would get his strength up and make them reap what they had sown. When Malachi pulled the plastic baggie out of his pocket, Dre took it out of his hand and walked out. The cool night air stung his face and almost made him turn around and go back inside. Almost. The thought of getting out of Malachi's grasp motivated him to keep going. He reached his arm around to his back and pulled out the gun that Tree had given him.

He examined the foreign object and then placed it back inside his waistband and took off down the street.

The traffic was light for a Friday but he knew that the fiends would still be lurking. He couldn't understand what they got out of getting high but he did know that he would never try to find out. With Tree's dope in one pocket and Malachi's dope in another, Dre posted up. He knew that he had to be careful because he didn't want Malachi to know he was still dealing another man's product. Dre was stuck inside his own thoughts when he heard a familiar voice.

"Sup, Dre? How's it going out here? What the money look like?"

He wanted to be angry at Kenny for not having his back when he approached him with the heroin but after the beating Malachi put on him, he was glad his friend didn't get involved. He would have never forgiven himself if something would have happened to Kenny and Tasha because of his choices.

"It's all good but I ain't been out here long," Dre stated and gave Kenny some dap.

"Yeah, but you know as soon as them crackheads realize you here, they gonna come running. You a celebrity to them."

"Man, I ain't no celebrity. They only fool with me because they know who my daddy is. I ain't shit to these fiends."

"Yo Dre, speaking of your daddy, when he coming home? Shouldn't he be out soon? Word on the street was he only had to do seventeen. So where he at?"

Dre looked at Kenny through saddened eyes. He wished that he had an answer but honestly, he didn't know shit about Daymion Myers. He had only been told bad things by his mother but according to the streets, his father was one of the greatest. He often thought about the visit he'd had with him and wished that he would have told him all that was going on but Kayla had come back from getting refreshments a little too soon and he didn't want to talk in front of her.

"I don't know when he get out but I know he gonna come get me, and I can't wait for him to take me away from all this."

"Yeah. I guess you really believe that. I just hope you know what you talking about because I'd hate to see you get let down."

Dre didn't like what Kenny had said. He knew that he was bitter about his own father abandoning him and Tasha but he had no right to think that Day would do the same thing. Dre believed in his father, even if no one else did. Before he could tell Kenny how he felt about his comment, Tasha walked up.

"Hey Dre. What y'all talking about?"

Kenny could only shake his head in disappointment because of the lust in his sister's eyes. He felt that one day, him and Dre would fall out about Tasha's feelings. He wasn't sure how he would deal with it when it happened but he'd be damned if he'd let her get hurt.

"We talking about his daddy coming home."

"Oh yeah. When is he coming? I can't wait to meet him. They say he was the king of the streets and the women flocked to him like flies on a pile of dog shit." She then smiled at Dre flirtatiously. "Don't worry Dre, you gonna be the king of the streets one day too and who knows, I just might agree to be your queen."

Kenny sucked his teeth and rolled his eyes at his sister's comment. He knew that Dre would never see her as anything more than a friend. He only wished that she could see it too. "Come on Tasha, we gotta get home. Sorry, but we can't hang out tonight."

"Ah come on, Kenny. We can hang just a little longer. Grandma ain't gonna care."

He gripped Tasha's arm and pulled her along. "No, we can't stay out here any longer. Now, let's go."

She knew not to argue with him so she complied. "See ya later, Dre."

"Yeah. See ya later." Once again his friends had abandoned him and left him on his own. He decided to stay out a little longer and then go in. Slowly, the bag of rocks emptied and his pockets swelled. He had sold all the heroin hours before and planned to stop at a phone and call Tree so he could give him his cash. He couldn't risk going home with extra money on him because Malachi would surely know that it came from someone else's pot.

When the last rock was gone, Dre took off and went to the abandoned house he had his stash buried behind. He counted his money to make sure all of it was still there. Satisfied with the outcome, he covered it back up and went to call Tree who answered on the first ring.

"Talk to me."

"Aye, this Spade. I need to come in."

"Aight. Tell me where you at and I'll come meet you."

Dre told him his location and fifteen minutes later, Tree pulled up. "Get in."

He opened the door and got inside the vehicle and emptied the pocket that held Tree's money and then he proceeded to get back out.

"Aye kid, where you going? Don't you want a ride to the crib."

"Uh uh. If Malachi sees you pull up with me, he might get suspicious."

"Let me worry about Malachi. I got you!"

Dre was skeptical but decided to ride anyway. He was tired and didn't really feel like walking home. His eyes were heavy and right before he closed them Tree spoke. "Aye, you want to stop and get something to eat. I know your ass is hungry. You can eat it on the way."

"Yeah, thanks."

Tree pulled into the twenty four hour McDonald's and ordered. He had to admit that he was a little famished too so he got enough for both of them. After they got their food, Tree made sure to drive slow so Dre would have time to enjoy his food. Deep inside, Tree had started to admire the kid. Dre was very wise to be seventeen, and he felt like it was due to the fact that he had practically raised himself. Kiara was a sorry excuse for a mother and with Daymion being locked away all of Dre's life, it caused him to have to man up before his time. However, in order for Tree's plan to work, he had to make sure his admiration was limited. He only needed Dre to trust him so when it was time to execute his plan, the kid would be none the wiser.

"Aight, we here. Just play it cool."

The two got out and walked inside together and Cardo was the first one to speak up. "Yo Tree, where you get that lil mufucka from? Y'all hanging out and shit now?"

"Aw nah, I was on my way here and saw his ass walking so I scooped him up and gave him a ride."

Malachi had grown suspicious of Tree and felt like he had been hiding something but he had no way of proving it. At least, not yet. "Well, how about next time you see him out there, let that mufucka walk. Unless of course, you got some business with him."

"Uh nah Mal, just thought I was doing a good thing. That's all."

Malachi stared deep into Tree's eyes to see if he could feel some tension. He knew that Dre had been out there selling product that came from someone else and something told him that Tree knew about it. He then turned this gaze to Dre and held out his hand. Dre reached in his pocket and pulled out the wad of cash that he had for Malachi.

"Good job kid. Now get the hell outta my face."

Dre turned and left the room but listened closely from behind his bedroom door, as Malachi talked to Tree. "Since you seem to care so much about his wellbeing, perhaps, you should warn him about how dire the consequences will get for him if he continues to sell product and put money in someone else's pockets. The person that gave it to him should be given that same message so see that it gets delivered."

Tree knew that Malachi said that last line to see if it would affect him but he wasn't no dumb nigga. "Do you have any idea who I'm supposed to deliver that message to besides him or are you implying something?"

"Hmmm. Just wanted to make sure the word got out there. I'm sure you can find out the source of my issue."

"Yeah Mal, you know I got you, and when I pinpoint who it is I'll be sure to deliver your message."

"You do that."

Tree's nose flared as he nodded his head at Malachi and Cardo and then turned to walk out. He hoped that he could execute his plan before he was found out. It wasn't that he was afraid but he didn't have an army behind him like Malachi did. He was still in the process of building his status and wanted to make sure no fingers pointed to him when the job was done. The kid was the perfect scapegoat. That was why it was so important to befriend him.

Tree jumped back into his ride and started the engine. He thought about Kiara and wondered if he could somehow pull her into his plan too. She was only loyal to Malachi by fault, and he felt like she could be easily persuaded to go against him. He would wait until Mal and Cardo were gone on a run and show back up. Once he offered Kiara the world, he felt like she would fall for it. She was desperate for love and that was something she'd never get in her situation.

Tree had plenty of love to give even if it wasn't real. The ringtone of his cell phone broke him from his thoughts. He looked down and saw that the caller was listed as unknown but he answered it anyway.

"Yeah, talk to me."

When the caller on the other end identified himself, Tree smiled because the person was another piece to his puzzle and he couldn't wait to put all the pieces together.

Chapter 5

"Day my man. It sure is good to see you, potna. When did you get out and why your ass ain't call me? I would have enjoyed coming to pick you up from that hell hole and telling them mufuckas to kiss my ass. You should have sent me word."

"It's all good, bruh. I ain't been home but a few days. I wanted to get myself situated before I reached out to anybody but here I go my nigga. What's up?"

Daymion had called the number Branch had given him and was elated when he answered. He couldn't wait to hook back up with his friend and hopefully make some power moves. He also knew that Branch would stand beside him when he went against Malachi Jensen and his crew. It wasn't that he couldn't handle things on his own but having extra muscle would help him get a better grip on the situation that he'd heard his son was in. He planned on keeping his return on the down low until he could gain some ground so he would need Branch to be his eyes and ears. When he did finally decide to show his face, it would be too late for a mufucka to take cover.

"So, what's your plans, Day? I got some work if you looking to be put on. Make ya some money and shit."

"Good looking out, B. I might actually take you up on that at a later time. Right now, I'm focused on finding that nigga who got my boy on blocks and shit. Ya heard anyone talking in the streets?"

Branch shook his head and thought for a minute before he responded. "Nah Day, I don't really fool with them corner boys but I can make a trip across town and see what they talking about. I been kinda staying low too since I been out. Ya know a nigga like me don't fool with that little shit. Mufucka gotta be pushing some G's my way just for me to even speak."

"Yeah, I completely understand but I need to figure out a way to make Malachi come out. I just gotta make sure he don't know that I'm the reason shit ain't gonna go his way anymore. Know what I mean?"

"Hell yeah and I know just how to pull him out."

Branch pulled out a gun and smiled. He had always had visions of running up in one of Malachi's stash houses but had yet to gain the courage to do so. He thought that Day's vendetta against him would be the key to the door and it would make both of their pockets fatter. Daymion watched Branch with scrunched eyebrows and asked. "What the fuck you pull that out for, bruh?"

"Don't nothing make a man move quicker than his money. We run up in one of those houses and he gonna have to come see about it. We can sit off in the cut and wait and when that nigga shows up, we follow his ass. He gonna lead us to where he rests his head and then we can plan our next move from there."

"I don't know man. If shit don't come out right and he finds out I'm free and had something to do with it, that could put Dre in some shit I might not be able to save him from in time. I can't take that chance."

"Aight. So, we mask up and slide through quietly. Nigga, we could take all them mufuckas out before they have a chance to pull out. We gon' leave 'em leaking and have they momma's and bitches planning funerals. Even if they did see our faces, who gon' report that shit back? Them niggas ain't gonna have no air left in they lungs to tell a damn thing."

Branch could tell that Daymion was thinking real hard about what he'd said. He only hoped that he had convinced him to agree to the plan.

"Aight B, I'm down. But if that shit backfires and something happens to my boy, I'm killing everybody in sight until I get to Malachi. Niggas ain't ready for the wrath I'm a put on this town if I don't find my son safe and sound. You hear what I'm saying, bruh?"

"Bet that, my nigga. My bullets gonna fly beside yours. I got your back, but look mane, right now, I got some shit I need to go handle but I'll get back up with you when I'm done. We can start sitting on one of them houses later and then plan our moves from there."

"Aight B, holla at me when you through handling your business and we'll get up."

The two men gave each other dap and then Branch pulled Day in for a man hug and walked away. Day stood there for a minute and tried to sort through how he felt. His gut told him that something about his friend was off but he couldn't quite place what it was. He wondered if Branch had his own beef with Malachi and his crew because of his eagerness to run up on his stash houses. Branch had never seemed like a jackboy to him so for him to want to rob someone made Day feel like his boy was desperate. Branch had promised him that when he got out he would find out all he could about Malachi and his resources but he had already been free for months and yet he knew nothing. To Day, that meant Branch wasn't a man of his word and when a nigga couldn't live by what he said, he shouldn't be living at all. Daymion had never said anything that someone could throw back in his face later. He only kept shit real. He couldn't wait to instill those same values in Dre. Real men backed up what they said and he would always stand by that. He decided to wait and see if his feelings about Branch subsided but he would make sure to watch him closely and if he showed any signs of disloyalty, he would be made to pay dearly.

The thought of hitting one of Malachi's houses was like music to his ears but because of the vibes he was getting from Branch, there was no way he would pull the move off beside him. Instead, he would scope things out and pull it off himself. The last thing he needed was an accomplice who could eventually turn on him.

Daymion decided to drive back to the apartment where he hoped Kaprice and Shay had finally called a truce. When he got there and walked inside, the sweet smell of free world food and the essence of a woman welcomed him. His dick instantly rocked up but he would have to wait to slide up in something wet, because his stomach had spoken. He followed the aroma into the small kitchen.

There, he found Kaprice as she stood in front of a stove and stirred a pot of greens. Daymion felt his stomach growl so he washed his hands and sat down at the center island.

Kaprice released a slight chuckle and turned around to face him. "I don't know what you're sitting down for. I only made enough for me."

"Oh yeah? Well if you ain't breathing, you ain't gonna be able to enjoy it."

"So, you gonna kill me for a plate of food? Ya know that's really fucked up right?"

"Nah. What's fucked up is how you ain't made me a plate yet. Ya know a nigga's hungry as a hostage."

"Damn. Now, that's hungry. Let me see what I can do for you."

Kaprice picked up a plate and loaded it with fried chicken, collard greens, baked macaroni and cheese and fresh homemade cornbread. She sat it down in front of him and smiled. "You're lucky I wanna live long enough to enjoy the finer things in life. Like that."

She pointed to his hard on and pursed her lips. Daymion had to admit, the bitch was bad but he wasn't on it like that. He smiled and took a bite of his food. "You better be glad this shit is on point or your ass ain't gonna enjoy a damn thing. And where the hell you learn to cook like this?"

She shrugged and smiled at him seductively. He didn't speak another word until his plate was empty and his stomach was full. That's when he realized that something was missing.

"Yo. Where the hell Shay at?"

"Hell if I know. That bitch took off shortly after you left and ain't been back since. Let her ass stay gone. Why is she here again?"

Daymion pushed his seat back and stood. "Look, I'm a need you two to get along. I need her on my side to help me find my son. All that bullshit you and her got going on over that piece of shit ass nigga has got to come to an end. Besides, ain't neither one of you running things up in here."

"Yeah? Well what makes you think that having her on your team will help you locate him any quicker? You don't even really know that bitch. What if she leads you into a pile of bullshit instead of to your boy? What you gonna do then?"

Daymion raised his eyebrows, "You too damn pretty to have such a foul mouth. Makes me feel like I need shut it up with your jealous ass."

"Ain't nobody jealous. I'd just hate to see a man like you get let down by anybody. What if she stabs you in the back? Or your son for that matter?"

"Hmmm, I guess that's a chance I'm willing to take. But remember, why you keep putting her down, I don't know you that well either and yet, I'm believing what you saying to me."

"Well, I'm different. I knew about you before you fucked around with Kiara Taylor's ass. I know the type of man you are Daymion and I know your boundaries. I'd be a damn fool to stab you in the back. I know the consequences."

"Do you really? Cause you trying real hard to get rid of Shay. Kinda makes me wonder why you trying to get me all alone."

"I can assure you, it's not to harm you."

Daymion shook his head and grabbed a cold bottle of water out of the refrigerator. He walked away and went to the living room where he sat down in front of the television. His mind went back to the talk he'd had with Branch. He wished that he could put his finger on what he felt because he just couldn't let it go, and then, his mind flipped to Malachi Jensen.

"Don't even think about it, Daymion. You'll never be able to pull it off."

He cut his eyes up at Shay as soon as he heard her voice. He could see why Dre would be smitten with the young lady and only hoped that the stars would fall in their favor.

"The fuck is you talking about?"

"I can see it in your eyes. I know that look because I've seen it in other people's eyes before and it will never work."

"Girl, your ass is tripping."

"Am I really? Tell me you're not sitting there thinking about running in and robbing Malachi's people because if you are, I'd advise you to rethink it and come up with another plan because if he finds out you had anything to do with it, you're signing a death wish and Dre's blood will be on your hands. I can assure you that he will torture him so choose your path wisely. I know him and he is a heartless bastard."

Day jumped up off the sofa and got in her face with an angered look. "Yeah, you know him like that? How the fuck you know him so well? You working with his ass or something? Huh? Did you put my son in his hands because bitch if I find out …"

"He's my father. That's why I know him. Malachi is my father."

The room grew eerily silent as Day tried to deal with what he'd heard. Shay had just threw him for a loop. "Don't fucking play with me like that. Let's just keep the shit real."

"I am, Daymion. Malachi is my father but that's not something I could change. He doesn't even know I'm his daughter. My mother sent me to live with my uncle when I was a baby because she was so young. She never told him or anybody else because she thought it would be safer. Malachi thinks I was stillborn. The doctors kept her secret because he was just as evil back then as he is now, and yet, she loved him so much that she almost had another baby by him but she was killed before she could give birth."

Day put his hands on his hips and scrunched his eyebrows. He thought about his words before he spoke them because he wasn't sure he wanted to speak at all. "Why didn't you tell me this before? Why did you wait?"

"Because I wasn't sure how you'd react to it, and also because I was still angry at you."

"Angry at me for what? Stop with all the suspense and just tell me everything because I don't got time for this shit."

"Malia Odom was my mother Daymion, and you killed her. I grew up hating you and told myself that when I got old enough and strong enough, I'd seek you out and when I found you, I was going to put a bullet between your eyes."

"So, what changed? You've had ample opportunity but I'm still breathing."

"What really happened is what changed. I found out that the bullet was meant for Dory but he pulled her in front of him and it struck her instead. I know now that it was an accident."

"So if you knew it was his fault, how the hell did you lie beside him at night? That's some foul shit."

"I just wanted to get close to him so I could eventually pay him back but I ended up catching feelings and couldn't do it. At least not until I caught wind of what he was doing to Dre."

Day reached out and quickly grabbed her by the throat. She understood his rage but the move was still uncalled for. She closed her eyes and listened, "If I find out that you went along with that nigga as a payback for what happened to Malia, you won't like the outcome, because the bullet that leaves the chamber will hit the right mark. I give you my word. So, you better tell me everything right now. It's your only chance to come clean."

He let her go and pushed her away from him but he wanted answers. He gave her a minute to catch her breath and listened to what she had to say. "There is nothing else to tell you. No more secrets. I only want to help you get to Dre even if that means sacrificing myself."

"Yeah, and how you gonna do that?"

She took a second before she answered. "I'm going to make myself known. He won't believe me at first but I know things that others don't. Things about my mother that only they shared, plus, DNA doesn't lie. It will get me in the door and on his good side and it will also get me close to Dre."

"Nah, I ain't sending you in there like that."

"It may be the only way. The safest way."

Day thought for a minute because he wasn't sure that he could trust her. He had only just met her and although her feelings for Dre's wellbeing seemed sincere, she could be full of shit and he wasn't sure he was willing to risk that.

"How do I know you won't go in and all of a sudden become soft hearted for Malachi?"

"Because I hate him and all that he represents. Just because he gave me life doesn't mean that his should be spared. He deserves every bit of bad karma that's coming to him. You will never have to worry about me siding with him. I give you my word."

"Yeah? Well, for your sake, your word better mean something. I'd hate to kill you and break my son's heart."

THUG OF SPADES 2 | COREY ROBINSON

Shay could see the seriousness of the situation in Daymion's eyes. She already knew not to cross him because she had heard how he got down and knew that he wouldn't spare her, not even for Dre's sake.

"I'm not going to do you dirty. I know you may feel like you can't trust me after what I just told you but I can assure you that I want Malachi just as bad as you. My mother was the one that loved him. I don't have those same feelings and there's no way I ever could."

"So, you willing to put your life on the line for Dre?"

"Yes, I am. There's nothing I wouldn't do for him. But don't try to rob Malachi, you'll never get away with it."

"Guess you really don't know me then."

About that time, Kaprice walked in and gave Shay an evil look. One that didn't faze the young girl at all. Shay didn't trust the bitch and felt like she had motives and if she was right, she would do all she could to expose her. The two women stared each other down but Shay was the first to speak.

"You should probably be more worried about her than me. Bitch is known to be disloyal when she's supposed to be holding someone down. A bitch like her gets desperate for attention and ain't no telling what she'll do."

"Fuck you, Shay. you're just mad that Dory liked me better. You was too immature for a man like him. He needed a seasoned woman, not a little girl just learning the ropes. Don't hate me because you couldn't keep up."

"Alright damn. You two 'bout to squash this bullshit or I'm a do it for y'all. We need to focus on Malachi and his set. I need to get to my son and if either of you got something else on your agenda, you can walk right now. What's it gonna be?"

Kaprice smacked her lips and crossed her arms over her chest like a teenage girl who couldn't have her way. It pissed

Daymion off to see her act so childishly but he would deal with that at another time.

"Okay, I'll let it go but Shay better not come at me sideways."

"She is the least of my concerns and as long as she don't hinder our efforts and get in the way, I'll be good. I got more important things to focus on besides her crabbish ass."

"Aight, that's good. Right now, we all need to get some rest so we can do this with a clear mind. Nothing needs to get in the way of the mission. Anything in the way will be eliminated, including attitudes."

Shay turned toward the door, "Well, I guess that's my clue to leave."

Kaprice spoke up before Shay walked out. "The couch is small but it pulls out into a bed. You can stay here. I'm sure that I have something you can sleep in."

Shay lifted an eyebrow at the gesture and decided to take her up on her offer. She was tired and didn't feel like driving back to her hotel room. Shay shrugged her shoulders and gave a slight smile. "Thanks. I'd really appreciate that. I'm so tired and I'm not sure if I'd make it very far on the road."

Kaprice turned and walked away but came back a couple of minutes later with a blanket, pillow and pajamas in her arms. She laid it on the couch and turned to Daymion. "You can crash in the room with me if you'd like. There's plenty of room."

Daymion shook his head and scoffed. He knew what would happen if he took Kaprice up on her offer. He thought about it and knew what he had to do. "Nah, I think I'll just crash in the recliner. We all need rest because we can't afford no fuck ups."

Kaprice shrugged her shoulders and left the room with a disappointed look on her face. She wanted to fuck Daymion Myers but he continued to turn her down. Shay laughed when Kaprice left the room. She appreciated her hospitality but she still didn't trust her.

"Why you turned her down? A man fresh out of prison. A piece of pussy is usually the first thing he looks for."

"Nah, pussy don't move me. Remember, that's what put me in the position I been in. Besides, I'm saving that first dip for someone special."

Shay smiled and lied down on the pull out bed and fell right to sleep. Daymion leaned back in the reclining chair but his mind was so heavy, he couldn't make contact with the sandman. So he just sat there and thought about all Shay said. He wasn't afraid of Malachi or anybody affiliated with him. He was going to hit one of his houses and leave his mark.

No one knew that he was a free man so that would work to his advantage.

He still wasn't comfortable with Branch and deep down, hoped his feelings was wrong, but felt like he would be disappointed in the end. As hard as he tried, he couldn't go to sleep. All the sleeping he had done in prison had caught up with him and kept him wide awake. He looked over at Shay who was sleeping peacefully and wondered if her and Dre really had a future together. He hoped that she didn't become weak once she was face to face with the man she claimed was her father. Dre needed someone loyal and if she turned out to be anything but, Daymion would kill her himself.

Daymion sat up and gave up on sleep because he knew it was a lost cause. He stood and as soon as he did, visions of the night he killed Malia ran through his mind. He had always felt bad about taking her life, even though it was an accident. He couldn't believe that her daughter was right there in his presence. Once he took Malachi out, Shay would have no one and once again, it would be because of him. He decided that he would take her under his wing as if she were his own child.

He wondered just how deep Dreighton's feelings were for her. Dre was still young but he was a Myers and knew what he wanted. Daymion would make sure that nothing got in the way of his son's future happiness. Once he rescued him from Malachi's hold, he vowed to protect him forever. He would give his life to save him.

With thoughts of vengeance in his head, Daymion got dressed in all black and slipped out quietly. He looked around but saw nothing out of the ordinary so he pulled the black hoodie over his head. He had one destination in mind, and he'd be damned if he let anyone stop him.

Chapter 6

The whirring of the ceiling fan wasn't enough to drown out the sounds that came from the other room and the cool air that it pushed out wasn't enough to keep Dre from dripping sweat. He lied as still as he could because he didn't want to make any noise. He didn't want to chance missing out on his opportunity because it may have been his only one. He had dreamed many nights of getting out from under Malachi and his goons but he had been too afraid to make a move. Now, Dre was tired of being afraid. If he wanted respect from anyone, he realized that he would have to take it. No one had his back at the end of the day so he would have to have his own.

When the moaning finally stopped, he sat up and wiped the sweat from his brow. He didn't want to move too quickly for fear of not succeeding in his mission. He couldn't afford to let anything mess it up. He stared at the room door and when his stomach growled, it pissed him off even more. Dre had grown tired of being hungry, not only for food but also for power. A power that came from having the Myers name. That night, he swore that he would eat and get full from both of the things he'd been lacking.

His days of being looked at as a pussy was over.

Dre reached under his mattress and pulled out the gun that Tree had given him and then stood. He held the piece in his hand and admired what it represented, power. He hadn't the slightest clue of how to shoot somebody but he knew he had to pull it off or face the dire consequences. Either kill or be killed were his only options and since Dre wasn't ready to die, someone else had to stand in his place.

With the gun at his side and his finger on the trigger, Dre walked out of his room. He could hear the light sounds of snoring and it made him shiver with anticipation. What he was about to do was needed. He had been given no other choice. It was time to represent the Myers name and his father's legacy. He had to show the world who ran shit. It was time to step out of his little boy shorts and put on his man jeans. Fuck everything else. Fear no longer gripped his heart because he didn't have one. It had been shattered since birth. There was only two people breathing that could put it back together but he had begun to feel like neither would ever come to his rescue, and he couldn't wait any longer to be saved, so it was time to save himself.

As he approached the door, he noticed that it had been left slightly ajar and peeked inside. One wrong move could end it all for him so he had to move smart and meticulously. As the moonlight shined bright and cast a glow over the one person he hated more than anything or anyone. Dre smiled evilly and pushed the door open even farther. The hinges creaked and stopped him in his tracks but when he noticed that it didn't disturb his enemies slumber, he carried on.

He stood at the side of the bed and stared at the figure that was hidden under the covers for a minute and then lifted his arm and aimed. He could only hope that things turned out as he had planned them or he could forget about his future. His hand shook and as hard as he tried he couldn't get rid of the nervous feeling in the pit of his stomach. His trigger finger itched but he could not get it to do the job he had assigned it. How had he gotten to that point? He was supposed to be in school and getting an education so he could one day be successful but instead, he spent his time on street corners pushing someone else's dope to the many fiends he didn't know. The only way he could think of to get out of the situation was to pull the trigger and yet, he was froze.

He closed his eyes for a brief second and as he started to lower the weapon, a sudden noise startled him. He opened his eyes back up quickly and without a second thought pulled the trigger and released all the rage and pain he had held inside. Once that first bullet struck, he knew there would be no turning back so he continued to shoot until the weapon had nothing else to give.

"Oh my God, no. You little bastard, what have you done? What the fuck is wrong with you? Somebody help me please. He's got a gun and he's going to kill me. Help me."

Kiara's voice brought Dre out of the trance that he had fell in. He looked at her and then at the man he had shot. He watched the blood as it flowed from the bullet holes and knew that there was no way the man would survive. He was about to claim victory over his enemy and then, he had got a good look at his victim. He couldn't believe what he saw and felt sick to his stomach. Cardo's eyes were wide open and stared back at him. Dre had sworn that he would never shed another tear over Malachi and his bullshit but at that moment, he could feel his eyes water. He watched Kiara pick up her phone and knew what she was about to do. He dropped the gun and ran because he'd be damned if he would allow them crackers to run in on him. He just hoped that he didn't run into Malachi on the way out.

"9-1-1, what is the state of your emergency?"

"Please help. I need an ambulance at 1422 Lackey Drive. Please hurry. He's been shot and I think he's dead."

Dre ran as fast as he could and left all he had known behind. He wasn't sure what they would do but he knew that he had to get as far away as he could. He thought about his father and wondered what he would have done in a situation like that. He didn't think about where he was headed but somehow he ended up on Miss Dot's front porch. He wasn't sure if he should knock or not so he just stood there and tried to catch his breath. All of a sudden the front door opened and Dre looked into Miss Dot's eyes. She was a wise old woman and he could do nothing but respect her. He wished many times that she was his grandma too but for some reason, luck had never been on his side.

"Hello Dreighton, you can come inside if you want."

Through labored breath he responded. "Thank you, Miss Dot. I won't stay too long. I just, I just need to see Kenny if it's okay."

"Go ahead. He's in his room."

Dre walked in and headed straight for the room door. He didn't bother to knock but instead, walked right in. Kenny looked at him and raised his eyebrows. "Aye man, what the hell happened to you? You ain't looking too good right now."

Dre made sure to shut the room door behind him because he didn't want Miss Dot to hear the conversation he was about to have with his friend. "I ran. I dropped that shit and ran but I got the wrong man."

"Yo, I have no clue what the hell you talking about. You dropped what and got what wrong man?"

"I don't know Kenny. I was just so tired of being up under Malachi and dealing with the shit he was putting me through. Tree man, Tree gave me a piece so I could put Mal's ass to rest and I had that shit all planned out but it wasn't him in the bed with my momma. I shot the wrong mufucka, bruh."

Dre didn't think about what he'd said until he had said it. He had always felt like he could trust Kenny but he had an aching feeling that he had trusted the wrong person. It was too late to take back what he'd said so when Kenny asked questions, he answered them truthfully.

"So nigga, who the hell did you shoot?"

"It was Cardo, I thought Malachi was in the bed with my momma so I waited until they were done and went to sleep. He was covered up and I raised the gun but I was about to change my mind. I heard a sound and got scared so I started shooting. I couldn't stop until the gun was empty but when that nigga's head came to light, it was Cardo looking back at me."

"Holy shit. What you gonna do now, Dre? You can't stay here with that kind of heat on you. My grandma would never allow it."

"How she gonna know unless you tell her? You 'pose to be my dawg man. You 'pose to have my fuckin back."

"Yeah, I am but ain't nothing I can do for you with that lingering over your head. You gotta leave man. I'm sorry. I ain't gonna say shit to nobody but you gotta go."

Dre could not believe his ears. His friend had turned him away and he had nowhere else to go. He stared death into Kenny's eyes and then turned his back to him without another word. When he walked out of the room, he ran directly into Miss Dot.

"Ya know son, I could help you if you let me."

"What you talking about, Miss Dot? I don't need no help with nothing. I can take care of myself. I been doing that shit all my life anyway."

"Why don't you stop trying to be grown and do grown up things? I know you ain't had the best life but you alive and that's all that should matter. Your daddy will be home soon and he's gonna be an angry man when he finds out all the things that your momma and her men have put you through, but you ain't gonna be able to spend no time with him if you on the run. Now, you go on in the bathroom and take you a shower. I'll get you something to put on out of Kenny's closet, and then you can sit down and get your belly full while we wait on someone to come talk to you."

"Why you always trying to help me out? I ain't your grandson. Why do you even care? And who the hell you gonna call over here? I ain't trying to get locked up, Miss Dot."

"Just trust me, son. Now, go do what I told you while I cook you a nice meal. We'll talk about it when you get yourself together. Go on."

Dre shrugged his shoulders and then turned to go do what he was told. His heart felt like it was about to beat out of his chest and he knew that he needed to calm down. He was too young to have so much on his mind but as soon as the hot water hit his body, he began to feel at ease. He wondered who Miss Dot was going to get to talk to him. What if he had set him up to get arrested and he had no way to escape? What would his father do when he found out? The sudden knock on the door brought him from his thoughts.

"Dreighton, son you need to hurry so you can eat something before your lawyer gets here."

Dre was confused because he didn't understand why he needed a lawyer. He hadn't planned on getting caught. He would run for the rest of his life if he had to and he would start as soon as he got dressed. Fuck eating, he'd figure that out later. Dre left the shower water running and got out. He dried off quickly, got dressed and then slowly opened the bathroom door. He stuck his head out and looked around but saw no one and felt like it was his chance to get the hell outta dodge. However, no sooner than he stepped out the door, Tasha walked up behind him.

"Why you creeping like that Dre?"

He turned to face her and put a finger over his lips. "Shhh, I need to get the hell out of here. I need you to cover me."

Tasha smiled at the thought of doing anything he asked regardless of what he'd done. She would defy Jesus if he'd asked her to because the only thing that mattered to her was making him happy.

"You know I got your back. Come on, let's get you out of here before grandma figures it out."

She grabbed his hand and began to lead him down the hall but only made it a few steps, Kenny had heard them whispering and knew what was about to happen and there was no way he'd let his sister get involved in a niggas bullshit, especially one she never had a chance with.

"Grandma, Dre's out of the shower," he hollered out loud.

Tasha was the first to speak up. "Kenny, what the hell are you doing? You're gonna get him locked up. You're supposed to be his friend. How you gonna do some shit like that?"

"Nah, sis, how the hell you gonna try to sneak him out of here? Dre don't give a damn about you. His ass is in love with Shay and you'll never stand a chance. In his eyes, you'll never stack up to her. I ain't about to let you go out like that. He dug his own grave so let him lie in it."

"First of all, you don't tell me what to do, and you're lying about Shay. I'm 'bout to prove my loyalty so he can realize I deserve to be the queen on his arm. Ain't that right, Dre?"

He didn't want to lie to her so he said nothing at all. Instead, he directed his words to Kenny, "You mufucka, you 'pose to be my man and you gonna switch out like that."

About that time, Miss Dot came into the hall with a man that Dre had never seen before. "Let's go, Dreighton. This man here is going to help you but you gotta turn yourself in. It's all over the news now and the police are looking for you. Just go with him and he will make sure you are done right by the system."

Dre looked around and saw that he had nowhere to run. He regretted even showing up there but it was too late to turn back. He looked at Kenny and before he walked out with the man, he said his peace. "One day I'm gonna make you remember this my nigga. I will be back so make sure you watch your steps because I will be tracking them."

Kenny's nose flared, a nervous habit he had acquired. He felt chills through his entire body because he knew that Dre meant what he said. He had admired Dre's courage from the very beginning, but eventually his admiration turned to jealousy. He wanted to be just like him but he would never be what Dre represented and that was a Myers. He had always heard stories about Daymion and the type of nigga he was on the streets.

The hood held mad respect for him and he knew that Dre was following in his steps. Daymion Myers was a boss whether he was locked away or not and Dre was lucky to have him as a father. Kenny had made Dre believe that his father was a legend too, but in reality, he was just a washed up crackhead who had done unthinkable things to get a fix. That was why Malice had always treated him and his sister like they were nobodies but he'd be damned if he let anyone else. Kenny knew that the man his grandmother had called would fight hard for Dre and get him the least amount of time he could. While he was gone, Kenny planned to get his weight up so he could be ready for whatever Dre had planned, but what he failed to realize was that word would get out about how he had switched up. Kenny would be on his own from that day forth, not even Tasha, his own sister would respect him. There was no room in the hood for a disloyal mufucka and that was just what Kenny had turned into.

Tasha would be the first one to let him know it. "I can't believe you wouldn't help him get away, Kenny. You just made me lose all respect for you. How you gonna be disloyal to him after all we've been through together? Dre knows our darkest secrets and he would never say anything to anyone about it. He would never sell us out. Malice was right about you. You're a pussy."

Whop! Kenny had slapped her before he even realized what he had done, and regretted it. He had vowed to always protect her and yet, he was the one who had hurt her. "I'm sorry, Tasha. I-I-I didn't mean to do that. I'm sorry."

Kenny watched as the tears formed in her eyes and he wished that he could take back what he had done. He was ashamed of himself because he felt like he was slowly becoming his father.

"I hate you Kenny, and when Dre comes back for you, I'm going to be right by his side when he gets his revenge. We are no longer family. Grandma would disown you if she knew what you did but since I ain't a snitch I won't say anything but just know from this day on, I don't have a brother anymore."

Tasha turned around and stormed away from him and although she said she wouldn't tell on him, somehow he knew that his grandmother would know. She had a way of picking up on things no one else could. The last thing he wanted to do was remind her of her only son, his father. So Kenny went into his room and packed a bag. He went to his stash spot in the floor and pulled out the bag that held the money he had been saving for a rainy day. That rainy day had finally come and it brought thunder and lightning with it. After he gathered what was needed, he quietly snuck out of his window. The next time anyone heard from him would be when he was ready. He would miss his grandma and sister but he had to go and prepare himself for the war he would have with Dreighton Myers, a war that he had brought on himself.

***

Dre sat in the seat of the car quietly but he needed to know just what the fuck was going on, where was the man that drove him taking him to? The man had said nothing to him and it had pissed him off even more. Dre wanted answers and was determined to get them.

"Where the hell you taking me to and who the hell are you?"

"Well, I can definitely tell you are Kiara's son just by your mouth alone, but you gonna talk to me with respect whether you want to or not. So, why don't you try again?"

Dre sat for a minute because he didn't like the answer the man had given him but he sucked it up and started over. "Who are you and where are you taking me to?"

"See, now that's much better. My name is Justin Valentine and I'm taking you to the county jail where you will turn yourself in for the murder of Cardell Jacobs. From there, you will be transferred to a juvenile center until the court decides whether or not you'll be charged as an adult but I'm going to make sure that doesn't happen."

"And what if I don't want to turn myself in?"

"Too bad, because you're going to. The entire police department has been out looking for you and the best thing for you to do is stop their hunt. I'll take care of things for you from there."

Dre smacked his lips and responded. "Why the hell do you care? I ain't nobody to you."

He looked at Dre disappointingly but answered his question anyway. "I care because your father is like family to me. I was best friends with his brother when he was murdered, but after it happened, I left town. I left Daymion to mourn the loss of him on his own. I was a fucking coward and was afraid that the killer would come after me next because me and Trey were so close. I never even checked on your pops after that even though I should have. Now I'm back and just wanna make things right between us."

"Yeah, well why didn't I ever know I had an uncle?"

"Maybe it's because you were raised by the wrong parent. Your mom really stuck it to your pops but he loved you just the same and he would never forgive me if I didn't at least try to get you out of the bullshit you've done got yourself in," he paused and then continued. "By the way, why were you still with your mother and not Daymion?"

"Since you so familiar with him, wouldn't you already know the answer to that? You know my daddy is in prison so why you ask me some shit like that?"

"Nah, playa, your pops got out a few days ago. You didn't know that?"

The tears formed in Dre's eyes because what he'd just heard felt like a stab in the gut. There was no way his father could be out and he was still alone unless what Kiara had told him was true. He could still hear her words as if she were standing in front of him. "Daymion don't want your little sorry ass. The last thing he wants or needs is a little crumb snatcher up under him and I can assure you, when he gets out, he ain't even gonna come look for you."

The silence caused Valentine to speak again. "Hey kid, you aight? Don't look so sad, that nigga is fucked up about you and probably knocking on doors trying to find you. Don't worry, when we take care of this. I'll locate him and let him know what's going on. I give you my word.

"If he was looking for me so hard he would have found me by now. He probably ain't even ask around because he should have found me the first day."

"Look, you gotta understand that although the majority of the hood was loyal to your pops, he still had enemies too. Daymion wasn't just gonna walk up and expect to rescue you. He had to move carefully so don't no one expected him because one wrong move and that could be fatal for him, or even you. Don't count him out, though. Mufuckas out there are afraid of Malachi Jensen. They know his name rings in even the darkest corners and your pops may be their only hope to get Jensen out of the way. I doubt that anyone even

THUG OF SPADES 2 | COREY ROBINSON

knows he's out and until he can locate you, he's going to keep it that way."

"So, how do you know he's out?"

"I'm a lawyer and we know things that other mufuckas don't. I asked the state to let me know the day of his release because I wanted to come back to town and try to make amends. I got love for Daymion as if he was my real brother and I don't want this shit between us to carry on any longer. Know what I'm saying?"

"Yeah, but how. You a lawyer and talk like a street nigga?"

"Like I said before, I used to roll with your uncle Trey but when he got murked, I backed up from the game and became something else, but just because I ain't in the streets no more don't mean the streets ain't in me. You starting out young just like your pops but I can bet you he would have never chose that life for you."

"Man, I was born to be a thug and I'm just keeping it real with my roots. Can't nobody stop my gangsta. Nobody."

"Yeah, well I guess we'll see how you feel about that once we get this charge off of you."

Valentine pulled into the parking lot and stopped at the front entrance. He popped the locks on the doors and then turned to Dre. "Aight, this is our stop. Just come in with me and let me handle everything from there. I'm a have to leave you behind but I promise I will be back. I'm a do my best to get you out of this shit, but you gotta work with me, aight."

"Yeah, just don't forget about me like everyone else."

"Nah, I got you and I'm a leave here and go see if I can find your pops. He gonna be pissed about you being in here but we got to do the right thing. The longer you would have stayed on the run, the worse it could have been. I'm a take care of you from here on out."

Dre's heartbeat sped up and it felt as if he would faint. He walked beside Valentine and stayed quiet while he listened to what was said.

"Hello, I'm attorney Justin Valentine and I am here with my client, Dreighton Myers. I understand that y'all have been looking for him so I brought him to turn himself in."

"Hold on sir, let me call the captain." The young lady behind the counter batted her long lashes at Valentine and picked up the phone. She spoke in a low tone for a few minutes and then hung up and smiled as she spoke. "He will be right out to assist you, sir. Can I help you with anything else?"

"Nah, that's all."

Valentine paid the flirting no mind because his only concern was the young man he had to hand over to the authorities. When the captain of the police force came out, he took Dre into custody. Valentine assured him that he would be back. He hated to leave the boy behind but it was the only option he had. When Dre was out of sight, Valentine walked out of the station and got into his car with one mission in mind.

He had been gone for a while but he always had ties to the blocks. He would seek out Daymion Myer and wouldn't stop until he found him. If Day was laying low like he thought he was, it would be hard to locate him so Valentine would have to give him a reason to surface and he knew just who to use to complete his mission.

Chapter 7

The gun that Daymion held in his hand felt foreign to him. It had been a long time since he'd held cold steel and he couldn't lie to himself, it felt damn good. He hadn't planned on using it unless of course someone gave him a reason to. Day had never considered himself a killer although he had taken a few lives. He'd always had triggermen to handle the bloody work because he felt like the boss should never have to get their hands dirty. Being out on the block felt surreal and even though he'd swore that he would never get back out there, it made him feel alive. He had been born and bred to be the king of the streets and he had always wore his crown proudly.

He sat there in the quiet of the night and thoughts of Trey came to his mind. He still couldn't believe that his brother had been murdered. It had happened so long ago and yet, it felt like yesterday. Trey had been his idol growing up and he would spend the rest of his life honoring his memory. He had always dreamed of avenging his death but he was sent to prison before he had a chance. He felt like he had let Trey down by not being the one who pulled the trigger on the nigga but when he heard the dude had finally resurfaced, he wanted it handled before he had a chance to disappear again. One of Day's most loyal soldiers had taken the job only to lose his own life in return. Day felt bad and vowed to take care of the man's family as soon as he touched back down but by the time he got out, they had moved away and left the past behind. He had heard nothing of them since.

A figure in the darkness caught his attention and he watched it closely. The figure was kinda small for a man and that intrigued him even more. Hopes of it being Dre entered his thoughts but he knew he wouldn't get that lucky. However, he would drill them and try to get some information. Day quietly stepped out of the car and crept up on the perpetrator. He grabbed his shirt and yanked him in the bushes he hid behind. The dude dropped the small bag he held in his hands and pissed in his pants. His eyes grew big as he held his hands up in surrender.

"Well one thing is for sure, you ain't mine. What the hell you out here doing this time of night?"

"Man I ain't gotta tell you shit. I 'ont know you."

"Yeah, you talking big shit for a mufucka who just pissed they pants. Now answer my fucking question, you little pussy."

"I'm just, I'm just, just trying to find a place to chill that's all. Me and my sister got into it and I dipped. I ain't doing shit."

Day looked down and noticed the bag that he had dropped. "What's in that bag?"

"Ain't nothing you need to worry about."

Daymion grabbed his shirt by the collar and pulled him closer. "Look, you little bitch. I'm a give you a chance to get that attitude in check and if you can't, I'm a check it for you. Now let's start over. What's in that bag?"

"My money man. It's my money but it's all I got to my name! You can have all of it. Just let me go."

"You don't look old enough to be out here with a bag of money all by yourself. You rob somebody?"

"Hell no. I ain't no damn jackboy. This my money. I earned it fair and square. And I'm eighteen so I'm old enough to do what I want to do. I don't gotta answer to no damn body."

"Who you running the blocks for because ya ass don't seem smart enough to run your own shit, and you better not lie."

Kenny hesitated because he didn't want to give away too much information. The man had asked too many questions already so he knew to be cautious. Cardo always told him that when a nigga asked a lot of questions that he better play dumb, because it was a jack move. He also told him that he'd kill his ass if he ever gave out his name. Kenny hated to think about his grandma having to plan a funeral so he quickly thought of an answer and hope that it was good enough.

"I 'ont run the blocks for nobody specific. I help everybody out when they need someone to do a run. They be breaking me off proper and I been stacking that bread so that one day I can boss up and do my own thang."

"Lil nigga, you look like you lying and you better hope that I don't ever find out different. I'm a go ahead and let your ass go but you better get the hell away from here. Don't let me see your ass again."

"Okay, I'ma go. I ain't gonna come back. I promise."

"Aye, I need to ask you something before I let you leave. I need to know if you seen a nigga around here named Dre?"

Kenny's heart skipped a beat because he wondered what the man wanted with Dre. He knew that his ex-best friend had killed Cardo and he couldn't be sure if the man in front of him was looking for vengeance or not. Kenny had already fucked Dre over enough by not helping him get away so he decided not to do anymore damage.

"Nah, I ain't never heard of nobody around here by that name. Maybe you should check in another hood."

"Yeah, I think I'll do that. Now, go on."

Kenny had been so nervous that he walked away without his bag of money but Day wasn't trying to beat a small timer out of what was rightfully his so he picked up the bag and called out to him before he got too far.

"Yo, ain't you forgetting something?"

Kenny stopped in his tracks and turned around. He was shocked to see the man holding out the bag for him to take. He knew right then that the man in front of him was unlike any other he'd ever met. He had expected the man to keep the money, not give it back to him. Growing up in the hood had shown Kenny a different way of life, and also introduced him to flaw ass mufuckas. He wasn't used to someone doing right by him and he was impressed. It made him feel bad about lying to him but it was too late to take it all back.

"Uh, thanks man." Kenny grabbed the bag out of Day's hand and took off down the street.

Day shook his head because he knew the young buck had fed him a bunch of lies. However, he also knew that their paths would cross again one day, and when it did, their encounter would be a little bit different. In the meantime, he needed to finish what he had set out to do. He got back in his ride so he could wait for his moment, but little did he know, it would come sooner than later.

Day gloved up as soon as he saw the S.U.V. pull into the driveway. He crouched lower in the seat to make sure he wasn't seen, and counted the niggas that got out of the vehicle and then he counted his bullets. He noticed the food bags in their hands which meant to him that they would be so focused on eating they wouldn't notice anything else. At least, not until it was too late. He waited patiently for them to walk in the house that he had been sitting on for hours. He knew that there wasn't anybody else inside because he would have seen them by then. He pulled the black mask over his face and exited the vehicle.

As he got closer to the house, he could hear the sounds of the Notorious B.I.G. rapping about a nasty girl. Daymion was a Tupac fan so he planned to silence the tunes of the enemy along with whoever else decided to run their dicksucker. Day had never been a jackboy but maybe it was time for a change. When he was running the streets, he had let so many niggas slide. Thinking back on it, he thought he was just keeping it gangsta but now he felt like those mufuckas looked at him like a pussy boy. His days of being nice and giving breaks were over and it was time to let everyone know it.

The steps felt as if they would crumble under his feet but he managed to make it up on the porch safely. He had thought about doing the respectful thing by knocking but since no one respected the Myers last name anymore, he'd changed his mind. He didn't go there to be friendly, but to show Malachi that his people can be touched. He wasn't in a rush so he was patient in all his movements. He first tried the doorknob and unsurprisingly it turned with ease under his hand. He carefully and quietly stepped inside with his finger on the trigger just in case a mufucka wanted to be a hero.

He walked the short distance to where he heard the music coming from and stopped only when the men came into view. It was only two of them and he watched as they stuffed their mouths with the food they had brought inside. They were so focused on the screen of the television that they didn't see the barrel of the gun until it was too late. He hit one of the men with the butt of the weapon and then quickly pointed the tip at the other one.

"Don't say a damn word or you won't make it out of this alive. You understand?"

The man nodded his head and then looked to his partner who had started to wake up from the blow. Day pulled out a small roll of duct tape and passed it to the one who was fully alert.

"Tape his ass up and you better not try no slick shit. Hurry up."

The man did as he said and then Day made him turn around so he could tape him up too. He could almost bet that the two men were mad at themselves for being caught off guard. They had been so busy eating and watching the porn on the television that he was able to slide right in. They had been so comfortable that they didn't even have their weapons close which made it hard to defend themselves.

The two men looked up at Daymion and wondered what he had come there for. He saw the look in their eyes and spoke his peace.

"I'm here for one reason only so don't add to that. I need to know where Malachi Jensen rests his head at. You tell me what I want, I leave you breathing. You don't cooperate and I'll send you straight to hell. Your choice."

He sat in front of them on the couch and waited but neither seemed to have anything to say.

"You niggas must think I'm playing with you. Now, I'm a give you one more chance to tell me what the fuck I wanna know."

Still, neither of the men spoke so Day decided to show them that he was serious. He sent a bullet to their knees and enjoyed watching their flesh bust open. The blood splattered on the carpet in front of them as they both cried out in pain. Finally, one decided to break when he noticed Day lift the gun again.

"Okay. Okay. Shit. Just don't shoot again. I'll tell you what you wanna know."

The other one turned to his partner and scolded him for what he was about to do. "Nigga, is you crazy? What you think that mufucka gonna do when he finds out you sold him out? Honestly, I'd rather face any gun as long as Mal's ass ain't holding it. He gonna kill you and anyone else affiliated with you so shut the fuck up. Beside man, where the fuck is your loyalty? That nigga been good to us."

"Fuck that, I ain't ready to die. Shit, Malachi got so many fucking enemies he ain't gonna know we said anything. We can blame that shit on someone else."

No sooner than he said it, Daymion put a bullet in his throat. He never really expected to be given the information he asked for because he hated snitches. A disloyal mufucka didn't deserve to keep breathing so he put him out of his own misery. He had failed the test.

He looked to the man that was left and raised his brows, but dude wasn't giving up a fuck thing. "Man, fuck you. Malachi been good to my ass. I ain't telling you shit. You shot the mufucka that was gonna give you what you wanted but you gon' have to kill me too. At least I'll know I died a loyal ass nigga. So, go head and do what you gotta do, bruh."

Day admired the man's loyalty to his boss and spared his life. It was hard to find niggas that stayed true to the game so when he did he gave them a thumbs up.

"You know man, you should be glad I took ya boy out. He vowed to live by the rules of the streets when he signed up for this life but he was about to break them. I don't know about you but a tell all ass nigga ain't got no room for respect in my book. That shit I just did was a test and he failed it. You shouldn't even be sad about it though. Mufucka would have sold you out one day too. A man can live by the gun all he wants to but he's got to realize that it's the same way he's going to die."

The man left alive wondered what Day had planned even though he didn't have anything to go on. "So, what now, bruh? You gonna leave me breathing and walk away like that?"

"Something like that but I don't plan on walking away empty handed. I'm a clean you out first and then leave you with a message for Malachi. You can tell that nigga that his worst enemy has risen and we will meet. If I gotta rob every house he owns until he shows his face, I will. I'm coming for mine so he better have his bitch ass ready."

Day left the thug in the living room and walked to the kitchen where he opened up the top of the deep freezer. The kilos of cocaine were stacked up like entrees but his interest wasn't in drugs. Day wanted paper that he didn't even have to break a sweat for. He moved some of the packaged meat and exposed two sealed boxes of money. He had done his homework before he showed up at that particular house so he knew everything that was in it before he even entered the front door.

He left the freezer food open and started to walk away but changed his mind at the last minute and pulled out the twelve kilos of cocaine. He found a shopping bag and filled it up with the drugs. He glanced at the thug one last time on his way out and reminded him to deliver the message to his nemesis.

"Aye playa, make sure you deliver that message and tell him thanks for the stash."

He walked back to his ride and put the boxes of money and bags of cocaine in the passenger seat. He knew that he was taking a chance by riding dirty but it was one he was willing to take at that moment. He drove carefully back to the apartment and hoped that the women were still asleep but his hopes were shattered when he walked in and locked eyes with Shay.

"You did it anyway, didn't you?"

Day walked past her without answering the question because honestly, he didn't owe her shit. Malachi Jensen had something that belonged to him and until it was safely returned he would continue to hit every house he owned until there was nothing left to take.

"Dammit. Do you know what you have done? If Malachi finds out that you're free right when his houses are getting robbed, he will put it together and when he does, he won't spare Dre. He will kill him and throw him to the wolves for dinner. Do you hear what I'm saying to you? What were you thinking?"

He turned to face her with a fire in his eyes that burned so fiercely it made her break out into a sweat. She backed away as he approached her, "Don't ever question my moves or tell me how and when to make them. That nigga has my son and this is the only way I can think of to bring his ass out of hiding. I don't have anything else to work with."

"I told you Day, you can use me as a bargaining tool. I'll give my life to save Dre's. That's just how much he means to me."

"Yeah, that's what you been saying but how do I know that when you see Jensen you won't go weak. I mean, that's your so-called father. You gonna lead him to the pit or are you gonna choose to turn rogue with him? I don't think I could trust that."

"I have no love for Malachi and he's only my father by blood. If I could have chosen who my father was I would have and it damn sure wouldn't have been him. You can't fault me or judge me by what he's done. I don't even carry his last name. My momma at least thought enough of me to give me hers. Please just trust me."

Daymion looked at her and tried to see if he could read deception in her face but either she was telling him the truth or she was a damn good liar. She was after all, the seed of Malachi Jensen. He decided to think about it while the night turned to day. He had to weigh his options which were very few.

"Look, I need to lay down for a few hours and we'll talk about it when I get up. I can't think straight right now, okay."

"Yeah, okay."

Day left Shay standing there and went into the bathroom to take a shower. He thought about what Dre must have went through while he had been gone. He knew that he had a lot of making up to do when they were reunited. He would give his life to protect his son and no amount of time could ever change that.

As the hot steamy water ran over his aching muscles, he felt someone else's presence and opened his eyes. Kaprice was kneeled down in front of him with nothing on but a smile. He wanted to tell her that she was wasting her time but before he could get the words out, she wrapped her lips around his dick. He let out a low moan and let her wet him up. The bitch could suck a mean dick and she had him on the brink of an orgasm in no time.

Daymion had to admit, a good nut would put him right to sleep so he didn't even attempt to stop her performance. As bad as he wanted some pussy, he knew that fucking her would be wrong. He had already gone too far by getting the head but the shit just felt too right. He felt himself about to explode and grabbed a handful of her hair. He pushed his dick deep inside her mouth and felt the back of her throat. He was ready to bust and the bitch in front of him was about to drink each and every drop. He gripped her hair even tighter, clenched his ass cheeks together and released all of his unborn down her throat.

Kaprice swallowed all of the hot liquid and then pulled away from him. "What the hell, Daymion?"

"What you mean? You invited yourself in this bitch so don't what the hell me."

"Yeah, but I didn't see you trying to stop me either. You need to come on and hit this pussy. I don't know what bitch you saving all that good meat for but I can assure you, she ain't gonna make you feel the way that I can."

Daymion looked at Kaprice with anger in his eyes. He knew that if he pushed dick up in the bitch, she would become a problem he didn't need. He watched as she leaned back in the tub and spread her legs. He could see the wetness from her pussy as it glistened in the light, but as hard as his dick was, he wasn't turned on by her actions. He reached down and grabbed her by the throat pulling her up to face

THUG OF SPADES 2 | COREY ROBINSON

him. He pushed her against the wall even though he swore that he would never put his hands on a woman. "You 'ont know shit about the bitch I'm saving this for, so tread lightly."

As soon as he let her go and stepped out of the water that was still running, Kaprice went off. "Ya know what? Leave. Have you forgotten that this is my shit you laying up in? I want you and that bitch Shay outta here and don't ever come back. You better hope I don't see Malachi before you do because I'm gonna tell him everything you got planned you motherfucker."

He couldn't believe that Kaprice had showed out like that when he wasn't even her nigga. She was someone he knew he couldn't trust and thought about killing her but he decided to chill on that for now. She was right. It was her shit that he had been laid up in so he would respect her wishes. He gathered what little belongings he had accumulated since being out. She watched with a saddened look in her eyes and knew that she had fucked up.

"Get up and get yourself together. We gettin' the hell up outta here."

Shay had already been awake from the commotion she had heard between Daymion and Kaprice, but she hadn't expected it to come to that. Without asking any questions, she got up off the couch and walked to the front door.

Kaprice tried hard to take back what she had done. To be honest, she was afraid to stay in the apartment by herself. "Daymion, I am so sorry. I didn't mean anything that I said. You don't have to leave. I would never run to Malachi and tell him anything. My feelings were hurt and I just got carried away. Please. I won't try you again. Just don't leave."

Daymion looked at her with disgust because the one thing he hated more than anything else was a weak ass bitch and Kaprice had definitely shown him her true colors. He started to say something else but the voices coming from the television ceased his words.

"Authorities have taken into custody seventeen-year-old Dreighton Myers for the murder of Cardell Jacobs, a known drug runner. Police say that Mr. Jacobs had been asleep when Myers walked into his bedroom and shot him in cold blood. When medics arrived on the scene, they found Jacobs had already fallen to his injuries and efforts to save him were fruitless. Justin Valentine, who is said to be representing Myers in this case has not commented on the crime or the possible outcome for his client. We will have more for you on this story as it develops. Back to you, Jim."

Daymion could not believe what he had heard. His son had been locked up for killing a mufucka, but at least he knew he was safe and off the streets. He wondered where Dre had gotten a gun and who had taught him to use it. He felt the anger as it built up in his heart and knew that somebody else was going to die, but it would be by his hands instead. Who had turned his son into a killer? He looked to Shay and passed her the bag he had been holding, and pulled out his cell phone. Once he called information and got the number he needed, he dialed another one and they answered on the first ring.

"Valentine."

"Where the hell is my son being held? I need to go see him."

"Ah Daymion, so good to hear from you. I had heard that you were out and have actually been trying to touch base with you."

"Look Val, I don't have time for all that small talk. I need to see Dre."

"Alright. He's down at the juvenile center so meet me there and I'll take you in with me. I'm on my way there now, and don't worry Day, he's in good hands with me."

"Yeah, well he better be."

Daymion looked at Shay and could see the concerned look in her eyes. He only hoped that it was genuine. He then looked at Kaprice and could tell that she felt bad for what she had said and how she had acted but it wasn't going to change his mind about laying his head there.

"Let's go, Shay. I got somewhere I need to be."

Kaprice tried once more to convince him to stay. "Daymion please, you really don't have to go. I'm sorry for my actions. I really am."

Daymion gave her the look of death and pushed her away from him. "I'd rather go back to prison and live in a cell than stay here. I don't have room in my life for disloyalty. I'm outta here."

Daymion walked out behind Shay and slammed the door in Kaprice's face. She was on her own and it was her own fault. All he wanted was to locate his son and get him out of the bullshit. He thought Kaprice was being generous and trying to help him until he could get on his feet but all she wanted to do was try and talk him out of some dick she truly wasn't ready for.

Him and Shay jumped in her car after he got all the drugs and money he had jacked out of the rental that he would leave with Kaprice. He didn't want to ride around in anything that was attached to her. He had the bread to go cop another one if he needed to.

Shay pushed the gas and sped to the juvenile center and as soon as she pulled in the parking lot, Daymion noticed Valentine as he got out of his ride. Seeing him made Daymion think of Trey and his heart ached. He still missed his brother but vowed to keep him forever alive in his thoughts and heart. Seeing Valentine after all those years and knowing how close he was to Trey, softened Day up. He got out of the car and walked up to him and as soon as he got close enough, Valentine pulled him in for a hug.

Day fell into the embrace because he couldn't lie, he needed that affection.

"Sup bro. It's good to see you after all these years. Damn man, you look just like him. Make me feel like he's still here standing with us."

"Yeah Val, I ain't gonna lie. I miss him so damn much."

"I know and I'm sorry that I didn't stay and be there for you. That shit was just something I couldn't handle but you and I both know they would have come for me next and I had to go."

"Nah Val, we good, I didn't understand at first but I do now. What's up with my boy, though?"

"Well, I've only been able to get a little out of him so I'm hoping that you can get him to talk."

"What's it looking like?"

"I'm going to try to keep the judge from charging him as an adult but if that happens, the prosecutor is going to push for him to be down until he's twenty one but that's the best I can get."

Daymion pursed his lips together and thought about what Valentine had told him. He had been gone for Dre's entire life and the thought of losing him for four more years was devastating but it was better than Dre being sent away as an adult for the rest of his life.

"Can I see him now? I just need to let him know that I'm a ride this shit with him."

"Yeah Day, come on."

The nervousness engulfed Daymion instantly but he knew that soon, it would all be gone. Valentine and him sat in the small conference room and waited for what felt like forever and when the door finally opened, Day's heart skipped a beat. His whole purpose for breathing had walked in and from that day on his life would be changed forever.

Chapter 8

The entire hood showed up for the funeral. Some came to mourn the loss of the fallen soldier while others came to rejoice in his demise. There would be an after party to celebrate the life that he had lived so even the fiends came to see his body as it lie in the casket. One would have been a fool not to show up for the free drugs, alcohol and pussy that would be given out afterwards. Everyone knew that Malachi knew how to entertain those that he thought were loyal to him.

Kiara stood in front of the casket and tried not to shed tears but she had cared deeply for Cardo. Although, she had to keep it a secret. Malachi had no one to blame but himself because he'd allowed Cardo to spend so much time with his woman. He had other bitches to tend to so to keep Kiara entertained he had to keep her with plenty of dick and money. The two things she loved the most.

The police presence was heavy due to all the hood bosses in attendance. One could never be too sure when the enemy would show its ugly face. One never could guess just how close the enemy had really been. Tree felt a small sense of relief for the killing of Cardo but he had given Dre the gun in hopes that he would kill Malachi. Leave it to a Myers to fuck something up. He was sure that the authorities would want to know where Dre had gotten the weapon and for some reason he felt confident that he would keep his mouth shut. He had no way to get to the kid to see what he had planned to say because of the rules the juvenile center had. He would have to be escorted in by an attorney. Tree was lost in his thoughts when Malachi's voice startled him.

"Well, my man, looks like I got a Lieutenant's spot open if you want it. But I need to know that I can trust you and your first job would be to find out where that lil mufucker got a weapon from."

Tree knew that Malachi was not fond of him so for him to offer a top spot in his organization had him skeptical. He felt like he was testing him and Tree knew that if he didn't pass it would be his ass in a casket next.

"Ya know Mal, I kind of like being my own boss so I think I'll pass on that spot. However, I will do my best to find out where the boy got that weapon from and when I find out, I'll bring they ass right to your door."

"Yeah, I'm a hold you to that. Now I gotta get back to business."

Malachi walked away but Tree felt in his gut that he would keep an eye on him. Tree had to be extra careful because he knew of the torture that Malachi's people used when someone betrayed him, and if he ever found out that Tree was responsible, he would kill him. He walked away from the casket and started to go to his vehicle. He needed to get away and try to clear his head but he didn't get very far before Malachi stopped him.

"Aye man, I'm a need you to take a ride with me. Two of my men are missing. I put orders out for the whole entire crew to be here and pay their respects but Crenshaw and Trell never showed up. I need to go over and see what's up with them two."

"Mal man, a nigga already got prior engagements so you gonna have to take someone else."

"Nah nigga, I'm takin' you. Whatever you got going on, cancel that shit. Now let's go."

Tree was smart enough not to test Malachi so he sucked it up and followed him to his car. He hoped that he wasn't walking into a setup because he had left his piece in the car, a mistake he had never made before. Tree had never learned to fight. Even when he was in prison he'd had others who protected him in exchange for sexual favors. He always played hard around others and no one ever found out about his secret life, and he wanted to keep it that way. No one spoke until they pulled up to the stash house that Crenshaw and Trell ran. Malachi was the first to speak.

"Aye, this shit don't feel right. Make sure y'all strap up."

Tree looked at Malachi. "Yo, my piece is in my ride at the funeral home. I ain't have it on me mane because I was trying to respect Cardo. You gonna have to let me hold something."

"Aight, go head and pull up that carpet and take your pick."

Tree lifted up the carpet in the floorboard and saw the small button on the side. He pushed it and the floor rolled back revealing an array of weapons. Tree pulled one out and shut the compartment back.

"Let's do this."

Malachi, Tree and two of his other soldiers got out and walked to the porch. Everything seemed quiet so they proceeded inside with caution. Slowly and with guns pointed, they walked down the hallway that led to the living room. The television had been left on and hard core porn was playing. One of the men was fixated on the woman that was bent over in front of a man ready to take what he had to offer but Malachi knocked him out of his trance quickly, and that's when Tree noticed a foot sticking out from the side of the sofa. He pointed and went to take a closer look.

"Mal, you got one down over here."

When the man's body came fully into view that's when he saw the other one. "Nigga it looks like you got two over here. One is definitely dead."

Malachi rushed over while his other two men went through the house. He knew off rip that Trell was dead because there was no way he could have survived a bullet to the throat. He put a finger to Crenshaw's neck and felt a pulse. "Hey, he's still alive. Help me sit him up so we can get this tape off of his wrists.

His other two soldiers came back into the living room and helped Malachi and Tree. As soon as Crenshaw was free from the tape, Malachi drilled him. "You wanna tell me why I'm finding you mufuckas like this?"

"Mal, look man, the nigga crept up on us. We was eating and that mufucka got us from behind. Wasn't shit we could do. I'm sorry man."

"What all was taken?"

"I 'ont know man. I been like this since last night, but he walked out of here with two boxes and a bag. I think he took it all. Mufucka ain't even ask where it was, he just went in like he already knew. Said to tell you that your enemy had risen and he was gonna rob all your spots until you gave him what you had of his. He ain't leave a name or nothing."

"So you mean to tell me a random mufucka just walked up in my shit and took over. How the hell are you still breathing and why didn't y'all fight back. That nigga shouldn't have been able to walk out of my shit with a damn thing."

"He-He-He spared me, said he didn't kill those that was loyal to their people even if it was the enemy. Said he admired loyal soldiers. He killed Trell because he was about to sell you out. Shot him right in the throat man. Wasn't shit I could do. He caught us off guard."

Malachi aimed his gun at the television and fired and then turned it on Crenshaw. His eyes grew wide and sweat formed on his brow.

"Nah, ya asses wasn't caught off guard. If you hadn't been in this bitch watching pussy you would have known the mufucka was there before he had a chance to get to you, make me feel like this shit was an inside job."

"Malachi, you know better than that. I been working for you for years and I ain't never did you dirty man. You know I don't get down like that."

"That's where you're wrong because I don't know shit."

Malachi fired a single shot between Crenshaw's eyes and put him down and then turned to his other two soldiers. "Burn this bitch down."

He walked out of the house with Tree behind him and got back in his ride with more on his mind than he'd planned on having. "A mufucka got to have lost his head to run up in my shit. They know not to try me like that, but I can't just put it on my soldiers. That shit is on Cardo too. It was his job to keep these houses in check but he was so busy fucking my bitch that he lost focus on what mattered."

"Ya know Malachi, you should be thankful he was in the bed with your bitch because I think that bullet may have been meant for you."

"Yeah, you think so? Huh? You might be right but it's hard to kill a nigga like me, know what I'm saying? These so-called gangstas out here been trying for years to take me out but bitch, I'm bulletproof. Ain't no stopping what I got going on and if you sitting beside me there won't be no stopping you either. So, come on man, join me."

"Yo, I already told you that I like being my own boss but I will help you find out who ran up in your shit."

"Good luck with that because I got a lot of enemies. I ain't never been able to narrow that shit down and now I'm just tired of trying."

"What about the boy's father? Ain't that mufucka 'pose to be free soon, if not already? I'm sure he has some type of vendetta."

Malachi looked over at Tree curiously because he felt like he was trying to tell him something. "What? You got some information I need to know about? Cause you damn sure know a lot for a man who ain't been out of the joint even a year yet."

"Nah, nah, man I'm just trying to help you figure this shit out that's all. I mean ya boy did say that the man said you had something that belonged to him. Kid tries to kill ya even though he got the wrong man and one of your houses gets cleaned out all within twenty four hours. I mean, shit ain't no coincidence."

"Well then, why don't get on the job and find out for me?"

"Don't worry, I'm on it, bruh. Just give me a day or two and I'll have all the answers you need."

Malachi dropped him back off at his ride and dipped so that he could check on his other houses. He had a funny feeling about Tree and would make sure to keep an eye on him. His instincts had never led him wrong and he doubted they were now. He would continue to try and convince Tree to be his right hand so that he could keep him up under him at least until he found out exactly what he was hiding.

Meanwhile, Tree thought about the offer that Malachi had given him and almost considered calling and telling him that he'd changed his mind. He knew that he had a better chance at pulling off his plans if he sat up under him. However, Tree wasn't playing fair on either side and knew that he had to be careful. If either team found out about his deceit, he wouldn't hesitate to kill him.

He thought about the house that Malachi took him to and wondered who ran up in it. He was pissed because he had intended to do the same thing and couldn't believe that someone beat him to it. Now, he would have to reconsider hitting any of the other houses because Malachi and his crew would be on high alert. With the murder of Cardo fresh in everybody's mind, everyone in the crew was angry. He couldn't believe the kid had actually done it. Tree hadn't planned on Dre getting arrested so soon. He had hoped that he could have gotten to Malachi first but with Kiara's big ass mouth and the hate for her own child, that she had bore, it had fucked everything up. Now he had to figure out just who he could use in Dre's place. No sooner than the thought entered his mind, he saw Kenny on the corner posted up. He smiled to himself and then pulled up in front of him and rolled down the window.

"Sup Kenny? Hey, get in for a minute. I need to holla at you."

Kenny hesitated at first but ended up getting in anyway and as soon as he closed the door, Tree spit his game and hoped that the young jit would take the bait.

Chapter 9

Daymion stood still and watched the officer through the small rectangle window on the door. It pierced his soul to see his only heir in the position that he was in. He was supposed to protect him from situations like that but he had been in his own situation and couldn't. His hate for Kiara grew even stronger because she had treated Dre like the enemy his entire life. He still couldn't believe that she had allowed something like that to happen and then to call the authorities on him made it feel like she had stabbed him and slowly turned the knife in his back.

His search for Malachi Jensen was far from over and Day swore that he would hit every house in the hood until Jensen showed his ugly face. No one would be able to calm the storm that Day was about to bestow. Innocent and guilty would all fall together until he got the hood justice he seeked for Dre. He could feel his son's pain even with a steel door between them and he vowed to take it all away no matter who suffered behind it.

When the door finally opened, Daymion walked in behind Valentine and sat down at the table across from his seed. Dre looked up at his father and showed no emotion. The hood had hardened him and his heart had even froze. His look caused Day to get chills all through his body. Dre's soul was black and empty so he knew that he would have to be patient with him. Dre was made to grow up and be a man before his time and although it wasn't fair, the damage had been done. The room was quiet and it was as if no one wanted to be the first to speak. However, Valentine broke through the silence.

"Dreighton, I brought your father to see you. Hopefully, it will make things a little easier for you."

"Yeah, thanks, but I'm good. I been doing this shit solo this whole time. I ain't asking for no one to come in and change it."

Daymion's heart broke but he refused to let it stop him. He couldn't blame Dre for being cold because he had never had anyone to give a fuck about him. Day had been away from him his entire life so he couldn't expect too much at first. He knew that he would have to earn his trust and he would do whatever he had to do to make that happen. He had to find a way to get through to him.

"Look son, I know you been out there by yourself your entire life but ya momma ain't give me much of a choice. I been looking for you ever since I got out but it ain't been easy. This ain't the life I had planned for you but I give you my word son. Everybody who had a hand in this is going to pay. I ain't gonna rest until them mufuckas feel your pain. Daymion Myers is back and I'm about to let the whole world know it."

Dre didn't respond to what his father said because to him it had all started to sound like bullshit. He felt like there was no one on his side. He had waited all of his young life to meet Daymion and when Kayla took him up to the prison he thought that all his troubles would soon disappear, but instead, things had got worse. He had heard Kayla promise Day that she would look out for him but she had been too busy to keep her word. After that, Dre had no more access to his father because Kiara damn sure wasn't going to make it happen, but he at least thought that Day would reach out to him. Dre just couldn't understand that Day would have moved heaven and earth for him.

The longer Day sat there, the more his heart broke. He could have sat there all day and told his seed what he was going to do but he knew he would have to get his ass up and show it. He held his head in the palms of his hands and prayed to a God he didn't believe in and then stood up. It was time to make some power moves and take back what had always been his.

"Listen to me, Dre. Even though I ain't been here by no fault of my own, I need you to believe in me. I need you to trust that I will always have your back. You the only reason that I'm still breathing. I love you son. You my fuckin heartbeat and if I could take back all the pain you been put through, I would. I'd carry that shit for you in a minute but if I got to eliminate everyone that crossed my path to convince you of that, I will. I'll be back for you. I give you my word but in the meantime, I need you to stay strong and keep your head up until you can join me out there. You a Myers and you can pull through anything. I'm outta here."

Daymion couldn't sit there and see his son like that any longer so he turned and walked out of the room. He had been on the verge of tears and the last thing he wanted was for Dre to see him weakened. He had to appear strong even when he wasn't and seeing Dre in that position made him more vulnerable. Yeah, Day wanted to kill Malachi Jensen and he would but there was one person he wanted to kill even more than that. He was going to make that bitch pay too. The hood wasn't ready for his return but they had better get ready because he was going in full force and there was nothing that could stop him.

Valentine let out a deep breath as soon as Day walked out. He knew what Day was capable of and didn't want him to do anything that would take him away from his seed again. He looked at Dre and saw the hardness in his eyes, but it was all a front. Seventeen was too young to have suffered so much. His heart had been broken and Valentine only hoped that it wasn't beyond repair.

"Don't worry, that man worships the ground you walk on. He will be back for you but don't hold against him what wasn't his fault. Keep ya head up. You a Myers and you gotta represent that to the fullest."

Valentine gathered his belongings and left the room. He knew that there was nothing he could do to stop Daymion's wrath. It was time for the hood to sit down because the king of the streets was back and ready to set shit straight. When Valentine walked outside of the juvenile center, Daymion was already in the car. He had waited patiently for Valentine but as soon as he saw him emerge, he got jittery.

"Come on man, take me to the hotel. I got some shit to handle."

"Daymion look, you need to chill and think this shit through. You still got connections and as bad as you wanna murder Malachi, I think you should reconsider and give someone else the job."

"Man fuck you. I ain't no mufuckin' pussy boy. I don't need someone else to handle my shit. This is between me and Jensen. That nigga gonna pay for what he got my son into and anybody who tries to stand in my way of that can get murked up too. I don't wanna hear nothing else about it, Val. My mind is made up and ain't shit you can say to change it."

"That boy in there needs you. Don't you think he's been through enough already? If shit don't go right I'm the one who is going to have to come back here and tell him. There's no way I could look in his eyes and tell him that you ain't never coming back."

"So, you saying you think I ain't gonna make it outta this alive, bruh? I was born for shit like this but you wouldn't know nothing about that, huh? Nah, cause you the type of mufucka that runs when shit gets to smelling too strong. But let me remind you of something. I ain't Trey and therefore, that means I don't need your ass. You a fucking coward

Valentine so go head and put your tail between your legs and go the other way because you don't stand for shit."

Valentine knew that he was right. Trey had been like a brother to him too but when Trey was gunned down, Valentine didn't stand in the mud. He never even tried to avenge his death but instead went the other way. Valentine had been a street nigga that was too weak to follow the rules. Mufuckas in the hood knew what they signed up for when they got into the game but Valentine had turned coward. He knew that he didn't deserve Daymion's respect because he hadn't earned in.

"Look man, I know that I fucked up. I got scared and ran and I've regretted that shit ever since but ain't nothing I can do to take it back."

"Ya see that's where you're wrong. You can make that shit up if you really want to."

"Yeah, and how do you suppose I do that?"

"You pull you guns and fight with me."

Valentine got quiet and thought about what Day had said. He wasn't sure exactly what kind of reaction to give. He had worked hard to become an attorney and let that street shit go but his past was coming back to haunt him. He had promised Daymion that he would always be there for him once Trey was killed but he had broken his promise. This would be his chance to make that up but was the risk worth it.

"What about Dreighton? Who's gonna be there for him if this don't go as planned?"

"Dreighton is a Myers and that lil nigga will live up to his name with or without guidance. This shit has to be handled and I ain't worried about losing my life because I got too many of them. I need you to stand beside me, Val. You riding or not because I ain't got time to keep sitting here talking. I got to start making moves. So, what's it gonna be?"

"Aight, Day. I got you. Let's take that nigga out."

"Now that's what I'm talking about."

Five hours later …

"Come on. Please just let me go with you. I've been waiting for this all my life."

Shay had been itching to get at Malachi but never had the chance. She had always wanted to use the fact that she was his daughter to lure him in but she couldn't lie, she had been scared as well. Her mother had only told her of the evil that Malachi held within. She had always asked her mother why she didn't just leave him alone and she always gave her the same answer. Malia was scared of him but she was also in love with him. She had been so young when Malachi got a hold of her and he had groomed her very well but when they had fallen out and she had ran to Dory, Malachi began to abuse her and use her for his own selfish game. When she came up pregnant again, she knew that she was stuck. She had been messing with Malachi and Dory but there was no doubt in her mind that Malachi was the father. Malia had decided to break things off with Dory and give Malachi a chance to be a father. Little did she know that Dory knew all along, so when the bullet that left Daymion's gun headed his way, he used Malia as a shield. He decided that if he couldn't have her then no one else could either, leaving Shay without a mother. Malia had been her everything and she had been sacrificed in a street war. She felt that it was time for someone else to be sacrificed. She had already left Dory for dead so she had one more target to hit and she'd be damned if she let Day stop her.

"You stay here because I'm not putting you in the line of fire. I owe you that much. I need someone who gives a fuck about my son to be around."

"You talking like you don't have any confidence in what you're about to do. If what they say about you is true, then you should be a little surer of yourself.

Daymion looked to Shay and thought about what she said. He had always been sure of everything he did but for some reason he felt a little put off. All he cared about was eliminating Malachi and his people so he could free his son from their grasp. If it took losing his own life in the process, then so be it. Dre was worth giving his last breath for and he was afraid that it might have actually come to that.

"I know what the streets say about me but you can't believe everything you hear."

"I think you're just saying that because you don't want me to know the truth but no matter what you say to me, it doesn't change the fact that the streets believe in you and you were once someone they looked up to. I don't see you letting them down."

"Well, the streets don't know that I'm back."

"It's not going to take long for word to get out. That's why you should let me go to my father and lure him to you. No one would ever know."

"My son would never forgive me if I put you in harm's way."

"So I'm supposed to just stay here locked away from everything?"

"Yep, at least until I can get the threat out of the way. Now, I have to go but I'll be back later to check on you and please do not go against what I've said. Just stay put."

"When can I go see Dre? I need to see that he is okay. You forgot that I'm the one who saved him from Dory's little brother. I'm sure seeing me would make him feel better."

"And how the hell do you know that?"

"Because I know him better than you."

The words cut Daymion like a knife but they were true. It seemed that everyone knew his son better than him but he would soon change that. He refused to respond to what Shay said and walked out of the room. He felt in his gut that Shay was going to defy him and figure out a way to get to Malachi and if she did, she was on her own.

Daymion rode through the hood slowly and carefully because patrol was heavy. He'd forgotten that he was supposed to meet up with Branch but was quickly reminded when his cell phone lit up. He wondered if Branch would ask him about the house he had hit. He would never admit it but he couldn't wait to see how he acted about it. Day answered his phone on the third ring.

"Sup, my nigga?"

"Sup, bruh? I been waiting to hear from you. Where you at?"

"Just refamiliarizing myself with the old blocks. What's up? You ready to make some moves?"

"Yeah, we need to meet up and talk about that."

"Just name the place and I'll be there."

Daymion waited for the location and then hung up. He could play cool around anyone which made a lot of people nervous. He didn't have a problem playing dumb with dummies and until he found out what was really up with Branch, that was how he would have to do it. Fifteen minutes later, Day pulled into the parking lot of a Holiday Inn. He looked around before he got out just to make sure that it wasn't a setup. When he saw that things were good, he got out and made his way to room 223. The door opened before he had a chance to knock and a thick redbone wearing only thongs and a bra appeared. When she turned around, Day noticed that her ass was so fat that the strap of the thong was completely immersed into her crack and it made his mouth water. She bent over when she got to the bed and kissed Branch while he lie back on a pillow. Her pussy print was fat and he could see her wetness as the cloth absorbed it. His dick instantly rocked up but he had to remember that pussy wasn't what he'd went there for.

"She ain't a bitch I claim, my nigga. So, if you want to wet ya dick up, you more than welcome. Ho got a good ass head game too, bruh. She'll suck the babies right out of your nut sack."

"Nah B, I ain't come here for all that. I'm here to discuss that business we got going on."

Branch slapped the redbone on her bare ass and then pointed to the door. She shrugged her shoulders and then gave Day a disappointing look. She finally gathered her things and walked out to go find the next baller to fuck with. As soon as she shut the door, Branch sat up in the bed and pulled out a blunt. He lit it and took a long slow pull and then stretched out his arm to hand it to Day.

"I'm good, B. Got to keep my mind on point. Know what I'm saying?"

"Yeah man but all work and no play ain't fun at all. A nigga ain't gonna pressure you, though."

"Thanks. Now, what's up with that move you talked about? I'm ready to start busting in doors. Shit, I need to get to Malachi as soon as possible."

"Yeah, I know what you saying but it seems that another mufucka beat us to it. Even took out one of his peeps. Know anything about that?

"The fuck is you implying?"

Branch let out a playful laugh but Day didn't find shit funny. He wanted an answer because he needed to know what the streets were saying. Branch took another pull of the blunt and then sat it in the ashtray before he said another word.

"Come on Day, I ain't implying a damn thing. I was just fucking with you. But on the real, they say Malachi is fucked up over that shit and ready to bust some skulls open behind it. Whoever it was took a lot of money and some keys, knew right where the shit was at too. Mufucker got a bounty out on whoever pulled that shit."

"So, what now? We still gonna move?"

"Shit, that's the first house I wanted to hit because it had the lease amount of men inside but that nigga got plenty more spots. We just gonna have to take one of those."

"Aight, so let's take one."

"I'm with you my man but we gonna need some real power behind us. I'm thinking semi's where the ammo don't ever run out. One missed shot and that's our asses."

"So, what we waiting on? Let's get that power."

"The gun power ain't no problem but who's going to come out of pocket for it?"

"Nigga, you been out all this time breaking bread but you can't put up the funds for some fire power? The fuck you been doing with your money? Shit, I'm just getting out from being behind the fence so I got an excuse. You been out long enough to be on top of the world."

Branch seemed to be embarrassed by what Day had said because it was true. He had his own thing going on and had been pulling in funds ever since he'd been home but he had tricked off a lot of it. He made just enough to keep himself with product. He was one of those poor ass niggas that tried to live a rich lifestyle. He refused to admit that to Day though, so instead, he lied.

"Now you know I had to invest some bread in a big deal about to go down. I put my money in shit that's gonna make me grow. So, we got to get the ammo another way."

Day knew that he was lying but he let on like he didn't have a clue. Branch had turned out to be a whole different person from the one he had chilled with in the pen. He didn't have his shit together at all and there was no way that Day would take a chance with someone like that. He would continue to do the jacks by himself.

"Look man, I got a couple of people I use to fuck with but I'm a have to go out of town to see them. It might take me a couple of weeks but it might be best to wait anyway. Mufuckas still on alert from that jack you just mentioned.

This will give things time to cool off. When they start to rest they hand that's when we'll make our move."

"Aight bruh, that's a bet. I hate having to put that shit on hold but you right. Let that other shit calm before we run in."

Day stood to leave and gave Branch some dap. He watched him pick the blunt back up and light it and shook his head. Day knew that when a man got high like that, he was never on point. He had just bought himself two weeks and before that time was up, he planned on finding out exactly who Branch was because he definitely wasn't the same. Day walked out of the hotel room and went to plan his next move. Eventually, he would hit the right one, the one that had Malachi inside.

Chapter 10

Shay watched the man through the front window of the restaurant. He felt so familiar to her and yet, he was still a stranger. She could see why her mother was so smitten because she had to admit, he was very handsome. It was so hard for her to believe that he could be so evil but she knew what she'd heard hadn't been rumors. Her mother had kept her away from him for a reason but she wasn't around anymore to stop her from meeting him.

Day had no right to tell her that she couldn't seek Malachi out. He was her father after all. She had only met Daymion Myers by chance and if it wasn't for Dre, she was sure that he would have gotten rid of her. She had begged him to let her draw Malachi out but he turned her down. However, Shay was grown and wasn't about to let someone else run her life. She had allowed Dory to do it for so long but now that she had eliminated Dory, she was free.

She checked out the woman who sat beside Malachi and wondered what part she played in his life. She wondered if he treated her the same way that he had done her mother. It really didn't matter though, because she wouldn't allow the woman to stop her either. She needed to get closer to Malachi to find what moves he would be making.

Day had signed a death wish by hitting his houses and Shay needed to make sure that Malachi had no idea who it was. She opened the door that led into the restaurant because she told herself that she was just going to walk up to his table and declare that she was his daughter. She almost made it to his table when another man walked up and sat down to join him.

Shay had seen the man before although it was only through a curtain but there was no mistaking that table and even he wouldn't know who she was but first she needed to be sure. She walked up a little closer so she could get a better look and when she realized that she had definitely been looking at the man she had seen with Day. She turned in her tracks and ran out of the establishment.

Day had no clue that he had been chilling with a snake all that time and she couldn't wait to tell him. She hurried back to the room that she had gotten for them and called him immediately. She didn't want to wait until he got back because she didn't know when that would be. The phone rang a few times and she started talking as soon as he picked up.

"Oh my God, Daymion. I need to talk to you. This can't wait. Please come back to the room. Please."

"Yo, yo, yo slow down. The fuck is wrong with you? Did something happen since I been gone? What's up?"

"You gotta come back to the room. I don't want to talk to you about this on the phone. Please just hurry and come back."

He could hear the seriousness in her voice and although he wanted to ride out and stake out another one of Malachi's houses, he turned around and headed back to the spot him and Shay had been staying in.

"Aight, just give me about ten minutes and I'll be there."

"Okay but please don't make any stops. Come right back here."

Day wondered what could be so urgent. He rushed back to the room and as soon as he got his key in the lock and opened the door, Shay started talking.

"That guy. He's down with Malachi. He's the enemy Daymion."

"Wait wait wait. Now slow down. What the hell are you talking about? What guy, Shay? Come at me correct."

"I remember some guy you were talking to when we were at the apartment with Kaprice. You had went outside in the parking lot but I looked through the curtains and saw him and then I saw him again tonight. He was with Malachi."

"How the fuck did you see someone with Malachi when I told your hard headed ass to stay put?"

"I tried but I couldn't stay put any longer. I went out to get something to eat and saw Malachi through the window of a restaurant. He was with some black lady and I was gonna walk inside and tell him who I was. I just wanted to get close so I could find out if he knows it was you who robbed him. Before I got to the table, the guy walked up and when I saw who it was I turned around and came back so I could warn you."

"Why in the hell would you go against what I say? The fuck is wrong with you? Are you trying to get yourself killed?"

"Ya know what Day, you should be thanking me because you been hanging with a snake. If I wouldn't have taken a chance and went out, you never would have known that."

"That man's name is Branch and ever since the first time we met up, I felt like something was off about him but I never would have guessed this. Are you sure?

"Yes, I'm positive, and they are probably still there because the waiter had just given them their menus. I could take you there so you can see for yourself.

Daymion thought about it for a minute and then decided to go check it out. He wanted to take Shay's car because Branch wasn't familiar with it. He didn't want to believe that his boy had been down with Malachi all along. He knew that he had been acting funny but he thought that maybe he was getting high off of his own supply. He couldn't lie, he would have rather found out that Branch was on Heroin instead of chilling with his worst enemy.

Shay pulled up right in front of the same window that she had been looking in. She pointed to the trio and when Day looked, he couldn't believe his eyes. Not only did he see Branch but he also saw the one bitch he hated more than anyone. Kiara sat proudly beside Malachi as if she didn't have a care in the world. Her son was sitting in a juvenile center for murder while she walked around happily with a bitch ass nigga. Daymion had the mind to walk in and yank her ass away from him but he knew better than to move too quick.

His blood boiled as he sat there and watched Branch break bread with his nemesis. He wondered just how long he had planned to play both sides of the fence. It looked as if Branch was comfortable with the company he was keeping so that meant that they had to have been real familiar with each other. Day's trigger finger had begun to itch because he felt like Branch knew where his son had been all along too and he didn't even have the decency to tell him. Day knew what he had to do now but he wanted it to be the right time.

"Start the car. We going back to the room."

"What? You have Malachi right there. Right where you can get to him. We can follow him when he leaves and then you can handle what you need to handle. Why do you wanna leave?"

"Start the damn car and let's get out of here. Don't question me as to why. Just do it."

Shay started the car and did as he told her. She had an attitude because she was pissed at what had happened. It may have been the only time that he could have caught Malachi off guard. She just couldn't understand why he didn't use it to his advantage. When they got back to the room, Day jumped out of the car and went right in the room. Shay sat in the car for a minute and then decided to get to the bottom of the reason they had left the restaurant without confronting Malachi.

When she walked in the room, she saw Day loading a gun and figured that was why they came back to the room. She gave him a minute and then asked, "Are we going back now?"

"No Shay, we're not. I just need a minute to think about this."

"A minute to think about what Daymion? You had him right where you wanted him. Hell, I could have handled his bitch while you took care of that bastard."

Day gave her a funny look and caused her to ask her next question.

"You know her don't you? I can see it in your eyes. Who is she Daymion?"

He swallowed the lump that was in his throat before he looked at Shay and responded. "Her name is Kiara and she is Dreighton's mother."

"Oh my God. Why didn't you say something before?"

"That bitch has treated my son like shit all of his life. That's the reason he is the way he is. She only kept him so she could use him to try and trap me but when I refused to marry her, she sent me to prison for rape. I was cool doing the time because I thought she would at least take care of my seed but instead she starved him and told him awful things about me to turn him against me. I met him for the first time my last year in there. I promised him that I would save him and I didn't. I didn't know where he was, but that mufucka had known all along and I'm a kill his ass for that."

"You're not going to tell him that you seen him, are you?"

"Nah, not at first. I'm a do a jack with his ass in one of Malachi's houses and then I'm a leave something behind so Malachi will know it was him."

"What are you going to leave behind?"

"I'm a leave his mufucking body."

"What are you gonna do about Dre's mother? You can't possibly spare her."

"Oh, Kiara is going to suffer for how she handled my seed but I want to save her for last."

"Are you gonna let me go to Malachi? Please. Once he finds out that I'm his daughter, I think that he will let his guard down and may be easier for you to get to."

He knew that Shay wasn't going to let up until he gave in. He wondered how Malachi would act once he found out he had a daughter. He remembered that Shay said she wouldn't get caught up in his web but that was her father after all and once she started spending time with him, Day was afraid that it would change.

"I still don't think that's a good idea. I'd hate for him to turn on you. Clearly, he has no feelings for anybody else and that may just include you too. I just don't think it's a chance you should take."

"Daymion, I'm going to Malachi with or without your blessing, so you might as well just accept that."

Day had to admit, the young girl was clearly stubborn and he knew that she meant what she said. He would do everything he could to protect her but if she veered away from him then there was nothing he could do. Her plan may have actually been a good one so he decided to give in to what she had asked.

"Look, I'm a go ahead and let you do this, but you better not betray me and my son because a bullet has no gender preference. If you fuck me over, not even Malachi will be able to save you. Do you understand?"

"Yes. Thanks, Daymion. I can't wait to set that motherfucker up."

"Aight, you drive to the restaurant, I'm a follow you but once you go inside, I gotta leave. I got some other shit to handle."

"You're going to hit another house while I have him distracted, aren't you?"

"The less you know Shay, the better off you are and the better you'll be able to play your role. Now, let's get moving and hope that they are still where we left them."

Day got in the car behind her and followed her back to the restaurant. He had other shit to do and didn't have time to stick around. Hopefully, Shay was smart enough to not go anywhere with Malachi. Day would have liked to stick around and see his reaction but if he was spotted, she could have very well been put in danger and he couldn't risk that.

Once she walked inside, Day pulled off and headed to the block. He was about to pull off another jack move and with Malachi busy, it would be the perfect time. The street lights were dim so he had a better chance of not being noticed. He backed into a parking spot and leaned his head back. Thoughts of Kiara came to his mind. Time had done her real dirty because she looked like she had lost herself long ago. He couldn't find it in his heart to feel bad for her, though. She had made her own way.

He thought back to when he'd first met her. She had to have been the most beautiful girl he had ever seen. He wished that he would have known then how ugly her inner being really was. He never could have regretted his time with her because he at least got his son out of the situation. That prison sentence had been worth every day that Dre had been on earth. He owed Kiara though, all those years that he had missed out on all because he didn't want to settle down with her. Pussy had got him fucked up in the worst way.

He saw movement out of the corner of his eye and lifted his head. He watched the female go inside the house and wondered if she was part of the set or if she was there for another reason. He waited to see how soon she would come back out and after about twenty minutes, she had still not exited the place. He wondered just what she was inside doing so instead of sitting there waiting for an answer, Day got out of the car and decided to go find out for himself.

Chapter 11

"Is there a reason why you are standing at my table staring at me?

Shay looked at Malachi through eyes like Malia. He stared back at her as if he had been hypnotized but not for long because Kiara had broken the stare.

"Bitch, my man asked you a question. Now you need to answer him because you about to be dismissed. Who the fuck are you anyway?

Shay ignored her and walked around the table to where Malachi was at. She had to get closer. The closeness caused Branch to stand up and put his hand on his weapon. He wanted Malachi to see that he would have his back and put a mufucka on they ass for him. Malachi stood too and stared deeper into her eyes. He felt like he had done it before because for some reason she seemed so familiar. Kiara watched the exchange and couldn't believe that he had the audacity to disrespect her with another bitch right in her face.

"Really Mal? You just gonna stand up and be all up in another bitch's face while I'm sitting right here beside you? You a real disrespectful motherfucker and I'm about sick of that shit."

"Kiara, shut the hell up and sit your ass down or leave, your choice. But just so you know if you walk out of here, don't bring your ass back."

"Fuck you Malachi," Kiara spat the words out quickly and then sat back down in the chair that she had stood up from. She should have been used to the blatant disrespect because it was an everyday issue. Malachi passed her from nigga to nigga and she could either be down with it or get the fuck out of his house. He didn't need a disobedient bitch in his life. He had always said that good pussy should be shared and Kiara was no exception to the rule, but he didn't mind replacing her.

Malachi focused back on the young beauty and could feel chills ride up his spine. She reminded him so much of someone but he just couldn't figure out who.

"Who the hell are you and why are you here bothering me? Did someone in my crew violate you or something? Just tell me and I'll take care of it immediately."

Shay was at a loss for words but she knew that she needed to find the strength to say something. She had not planned for things to go the way that they did but Day had been right. She could feel her heart soften in his presence. She was positive that her mother had felt the same way. She could see how easy it was to get a sense of weakness around him. However, she knew that he had to snap out of it so she took a deep breath and said what she had went there to say.

"My name is Monshay Odom and I'm your daughter, Malachi."

The words hit him like a bullet to the chest. He couldn't believe that the young woman had the audacity to walk up to him and make such a claim. Malachi hadn't fathered any children in years. The first seed he had planted died at birth and the second died in the mother's stomach after a deadly shooting. He had always taken precautions before he wet his dick up so there was no way he could have slipped. The girl in front of him had to be around eighteen or nineteen and he felt like it was some kind of setup.

After his first love had been killed by Daymion Myers, he vowed to never give his heart to another and he had kept that vow all his life. He didn't have time for the games that the female was playing so he decided to set her straight.

"How dare you walk up in here and claim to be a child of mine. I make sure that I don't leave seeds planted. So, what the hell do you really want because I'm out of patience."

"It's not a joke, Malachi. You are my father. My mother lied to you and told you that I didn't make it when I was born but I did. She was afraid that because of the life you lived it would affect me in some type of way too. She sent me to live with her family so that I would be safe."

"Oh yeah. Well that's a good ass story but I still don't believe you. Now you gonna have to come better than that because your ass is about to eat a bullet."

"Malia was my mother. I wasn't stillborn like she had said. I was healthy as any newborn could be. She lied to you, Malachi. I am your daughter."

Malachi sat back down in his chair so that he could absorb all that she had told him. The mention of Malia's name stabbed him right in the chest. He had never been the best man but he truly had loved her. He knew that he would never find another woman like her so he had gave up trying long ago. He thought back to when things were right between them. They were so young and in love. He was only twenty years old and she had been thirteen but they vowed to spend the rest of their lives together. Malachi had been just as ruthless back then as he was now. He had lived the life of a thug all of his life and had been raised around nothing but killers. It was all that he had known.

Malia's parents did not approve of their relationship so when she came up pregnant they were sure that it would cause problems. They parted ways and Malia was left to hide her pregnancy the best she could. By the time her parents found out about it, she was too far along for them to make her get rid of it. They questioned her daily about the father's identity but Malia refused to sell Malachi out. Their time away from each other changed the both of them. Malachi became even more violent and when bodies started to drop in the neighborhood, Malia knew that it was by his hands. The time had also made her grow lonely and that is when she met Dorian Thompson known to the hood as Dory.

Dory's level of street status may not have been as high as Malachi's but he was a baller just the same and for some reason, Malia knew that she only belonged with ballers. Dory had also been younger than Malachi so she knew that she wouldn't have to worry about her parents. However, they became the least of her worries. When Malachi found out about their relationship, he was ready to take Dory out but Malia convinced him otherwise. She told him that she would use Dory and make her parents believe that he was the child's father. Her parents became fond of Dory because of his low key attitude and they thought that he treated their daughter well. However, their relationship only lasted a few months because Dory felt like he was too young to settle with just one girl, especially one that was about to have another nigga's seed.

Malachi's growing violent ways and ill temper caused Malia to fear him so when her due date neared, she decided that he had no place in the child's life. She would do all that she could to protect the daughter that she had carried for nine months. She ultimately promised the doctor sexual favors in exchange for a fake death certificate so she could show it to Malachi. If he thought the child was stillborn and didn't make it, he would never look for her. Together, they would mourn the loss of their daughter. When their grieving process was over, Malachi became distant for a while and Malia ran back to Dory although he had other women on the side.

Malia had hated to pass her new baby girl off to someone else to raise but she wanted the child to have a chance at having a better life and being somebody. She would often visit and tell little Monshay stories of her father. However, not all the stories were good. Malia wanted her child to know the truth about Malachi Jensen because to keep it from her would have been unfair. Malia tried so hard to leave Malachi alone but he was her weakness although she still spent time with Dory too.

When Shay was nine years old, Malia became pregnant again and even though she had been sleeping with both men, she knew without a doubt that it was Malachi's son she carried. Dory knew it too but pretended that all was good between them until his enemy came out of the woods. Him and Daymion Myers had been beefing for the longest time and when the enemy came looking for him, he used Malia and her unborn son as a shield. Her and her child died instantly leaving young Shay without a mother and Malachi Jensen with a broken heart. He had not been the same since.

Malachi looked up at the young woman again and stared deep into her eyes. He could feel Malia's presence and stood up again. Kiara stood too and grabbed her purse with an attitude.

"Are you really gonna believe this bitch, Malachi? She is obviously trying to get some money out of you so just give her a couple of stacks and send that ho on her way. I'm sick of looking at her. Do you hear me, Malachi?"

Malachi tried to ignore Kiara but it was hard to do. He was interested in the young girl's story but he still had some doubts. He needed to know more but with Kiara's bitch ass behind him running her mouth, it would end up being a distraction. He decided to get rid of her. He looked at Branch, the man he had known as Tree and gave him the task of eliminating his problem.

"Aye playa, can you take this bitch somewhere so she can get the fuck outta my ear? Shit's starting to piss me off and about to cause me to make a scene."

"Yeah, Mal, I got you man. Let's go Kiara."

"Fuck you. I ain't going no damn where with you. I'm a stay my ass right here and find out just what the hell is up with this bullshit ass story this ho done walked up and told."

Malachi's nose flared, a habit he had when he was on the verge of killing someone. Kiara was really just another piece of pussy to him so for her to think that she was just gonna talk to him any kind of way pissed him off. No sooner than the words left her dick sucking lips, he turned around and wrapped his hand around her small throat. He had always told her that she had the perfect neck for choking out, but now he was about to show her.

"Bitch, I'm a tell you one more time to get the fuck on. I don't need that bullshit you spitting so if you wanna wake up tomorrow, you will walk out that door and let him take you home. This is your last mufucking chance."

When he let her go, she coughed and rubbed her throat but didn't say one word. She knew that he meant what he said so she had no other choice but to leave with Tree. She wanted so badly to cry but she refused to let Malachi or the woman who claimed to be his daughter see her so weak.

"Fine, I'll leave but don't get mad when you get home later and I ain't there to suck your damn dick, you piece of shit," and then she stormed out.

Malachi gestured to an empty seat and Shay sat down. After he summoned the waiter, he sat down too. He stared at her but said nothing. He had so many questions but wasn't sure where to start. He thought the situation was still too good to be true but he would deal with that later.

"So, if you're my daughter and you've known that all your life, why did you wait so long to find me?"

"That's a fair question and I'll be honest with you. I was afraid, Malachi. My mother told me a lot of wonderful things about you but she also told me the bad things. You're a killer and your name rings deep in the streets. I guess I just wasn't sure that you would believe me."

"Just how old are you?"

"I just turned nineteen. I guess you want to do the math but you don't have to. We can do the whole paternity DNA thing if you want but I am your daughter and it's just something you'll have to accept. I can't change that fact. However, if you don't want anything to do with me, I'll understand and I'll walk out of here and never bother you again. Just say the word and I'm gone."

"No, that's not what I want. This is just something I gotta get used to so bear with me. I been a hard ass nigga all my life so I ain't use to giving a fuck about nobody but me. I loved one woman and that was Malia so I just need you to understand that this is some shit that's new to me."

The waiter came back with their order but neither touched their food. They were too hyped up about the situation. They sat and talked for a little over an hour until Malachi's phone rang. He didn't even bother to look at the caller ID, something he had always done but Shay had thrown him completely off his game.

"Yeah, what's up?"

The caller spoke into the phone as Malachi listened intently. The call seemed serious so Shay just sat back and finished the drink she had been nursing. When Malachi disconnected the call, he had a disturbed look on his face.

"I hate to do this but I gotta get outta here. Got a little issue with one of my drivers so I need to go handle it. However, I don't want this to be the last time I see you. We have a lot of catching up to do if you cool with that."

"I wouldn't be here if I wasn't. Thanks for believing me but we can still get the DNA test if you want. That may actually make you feel more comfortable."

"Yeah, we can do that. Just let me know when and where and I'll be there."

Shay smiled and then Malachi turned and walked out. She knew that she had him where she wanted him and couldn't wait to tell Day what had happened. He would be happy because it would get him one step closer to his target. She walked outside of the restaurant and started to get in her car but before she opened the door, Kiara came from nowhere and ran up on her.

"Bitch, I don't know who in the hell you are but if you think you're just gonna prance your ass into Malachi's life and push me out you're crazy. I've bowed down to that nigga for a while just to earn my spot and I'll be damned if I let you walk in and take it."

"Look, I don't know what you think I'm trying to do but whatever it is, you are obviously scared and you have good reason to be, but if you don't want to be eliminated out of Malachi's life for good then I suggest you continue to bow down bitch. I'm his daughter and if you think he would choose you over me you're just as crazy as you look. If you don't want me to make him choose, then I suggest you stay in your fucking place. Now get the hell outta my way."

Kiara moved out of her way and Shay got in her car. She started the engine and gave Kiara one last glance before she pulled off. She tried to imagine just how her father could put up with someone so vicious but she had to remember that he was the same way. She decided that if Kiara got in the way of her ultimate plan she would eliminate her herself. After all, she was her father's child.

As soon as she walked into the room, Day jumped up out of the chair he had been sitting in. He had waited patiently for her return after he had gotten back from his stake out. He had started to get worried and had thought about going back to the restaurant to see just what was up but seeing her walk in safely ease that burden.

"What the hell was you trying to do, stay all night? You had me fucking worried. I knew that shit wasn't a good idea."

"Relax, Daymion, you don't have to worry about Malachi harming me. He was so happy to find out that I was his daughter and he didn't believe me at first but I told him intimate things about him and my mother giving him no other choice. I even agreed to a DNA test even though he said it wasn't necessary. He won't be a problem at all but his bitch on the other hand is going to be an issue. How the hell did you mess with someone like that?"

"Hmm, sometimes I ask myself that but when I think of Dre, it makes it all worth it. Did she give you a problem with Malachi there?"

"Oh yeah, but he made her ass leave. Somehow though, she came back and approached me as I was leaving. I'm going to have to get rid of her if I want this to work."

"Nah, you let me take care of Kiara. I owe that bitch for all those years I lost with my son. She ain't gonna cause you no problems, not as long as I'm breathing. Now, tell me what you plan on doing from here."

"Me and Malachi are going to meet up to take a DNA test. It's what I want to do because it's one thing to hear you have a daughter but it's a whole other thing to see the proof with your own eyes. We got him, Daymion. I told you that you didn't have to worry."

"Yeah, you say that now but once you start spending that time with him you may change what you saying. I don't want to have to kill you Shay but you need to know that I will not hesitate if you betray me and my son. I won't think twice about your life. So you better make sure you can pull through your end of this."

The words he said brought chill bumps all over her skin. She knew that he meant what he said. Shay had no intentions of being disloyal. She cared too much for Dre to do that. True enough, Malachi touched a place inside of her that only her mother had ever seen but she declared that she would be strong enough to fight it. Malachi Jensen would never be able to weaken her. That's what she told herself. She could only hope that it was true.

Chapter 12

If Daymion wanted to find out more about what Branch had been doing then he would have to find another source. Dre was no snitch and not even his own father could convince him to speak up. Day knew that it would be hard to earn his trust but he didn't mind putting in the work to do it. He had to admit that he was real proud of him. Dre had stood strong even through the worst of circumstances.

Valentine had already informed him that the judge wouldn't try him as an adult but he would lock him up until his twenty-first birthday. The words had cut Day like a knife but there was nothing he could do about it. He would just have to ride the time with him and hoped he grew up to be a better man. However, Day knew that Dre would come out stronger than ever because he knew the type of boys that would be doing the time with him. For some reason, he felt like Dre could stand up to the toughest of them.

Valentine promised him that after Dre was sentenced and he was done with the case, he would join forces with him and help fight his street battle. After all, he owed him that much. However, Valentine had made promises before and failed to pull through. Instead, he had dipped on him like a pussy ass coward. Valentine had been Trey's best friend and Day looked up to him like a surrogate brother because they had all been through so much together. When Trey had been violently killed in a street beef, Valentine vowed to step up and be there but he had disappeared and left Day to fend for himself. With Valentine showing up after being gone for so many years, it made Day skeptical. He wondered why he had really came back and hoped that it was for all the right reasons.

Day left the juvenile center with a heavy heart. His trigger finger itched so bad it made his dick rock the fuck up. He couldn't believe that he had hung out with Branch for years in the pen and he never once mentioned that he was down with Malachi's crew. That mufucka had known where Dre was at and never said anything. He had Day convinced that he gave a fuck when all along he could have cared less. He used Dre for his own selfish gain and because of that he would have to die.

Day pulled down the street from the trap house he had sat on for two nights. He had heard that it was one that Malachi frequented the most but he had yet to see him. He wondered why the nigga went to it so much but when Day saw the black beauty walk outside and get into the Lexus jeep, he answered his own question. He wondered just who else had been inside but he didn't have to wait long to find out. A nigga in nothing but a pair of boxers walked out and checked the mailbox. When he pulled out six small square packages, Day knew exactly what it was. He smiled a half smile because he realized that Malachi was actually smarter than he thought. What better way to deliver drugs to your workers and not be seen especially when you thought a mufucka was after you. It didn't matter how Malachi moved, they would soon cross paths anyway and Daymion would be ready. He remembered the anger he felt when he saw Malachi and Kiara in that restaurant together. He wanted to blow the entire place up but he knew that he had to be rational because his son needed him, seeing Branch break bread with them made his blood boil even higher. That was supposed to be his boy and he had betrayed Day in the worst way. They had made plans to do big things once the both of them were free but Branch had to go and fuck things up.

Daymion pulled on his black gloves and then slid the mask down over his face. He picked the gun up from off the seat beside him and made sure that it was ready to smoke a mufucka. He pulled the latch on the door and was about to get out when another vehicle pulled up and stopped him. The ride looked familiar to him and when Kaprice stepped out, he almost shit on himself. He couldn't believe his luck. She looked around nervously as if she knew someone was watching her, but she never would have guessed it was him. He had known in his gut that the bitch was grimy but he tried to give her the benefit of the doubt.

He waited patiently for her to go inside the house and then slowly made his way behind her. He watched through the window as she undressed and allowed the man to grope her breasts. It made Daymion sick to his stomach to think that the bitch had been sweating his jock not too long ago. He knew that she was a disloyal bitch but she had betrayed the wrong mufucka. He decided that since he had no intention of sparing either one of them, he would go in without the mask. He wanted Kaprice to look him in the eyes when he busted her heart open. He watched the man lie back on the couch and when he did, Kaprice mounted him. That is when Daymion decided to make his move.

He tried the doorknob and found it locked but he had learned how to pick one in prison. It was crazy to think that you were supposed to get some kind of rehabilitation when you were locked up but instead, you learned how to commit a better crime. Day had been a drug dealer all his life, not a man who committed B and E's and yet, there he was, breaking in on a couple who was only trying to get a nut.

When he heard the lock click, he smiled at his accomplishment. He knew they hadn't heard him because she was moaning and crying out like he was digging her a new hole. He walked quietly and slowly to the living room and watched as Kaprice rode the nigga like he had the last dick on earth. Day had to admit that the bitch had some good head but it wasn't enough for him to spare her.

"Oh shit, Gun. I'm about to cum baby. Yes, mmm, hmmm, yes. Keep giving me this good dick, Gun. You making me cum. Yes, I'm cumming."

"That's right, baby girl. Dory ain't never gave you dick like this. That crippled ass mufucka couldn't make you cum but you can cum on this mufucka. Go ahead and wet this dick up. Make a nigga wanna shoot off all in that pussy. Yeah, just like that."

Day decided that he would wait and let them get a nut. He figured that was the least he could do since he planned on taking them out. What better way to go than happy and satisfied? He wouldn't have to wait long, though. He heard one last grunt come from the man and then he went stiff beneath her. That's when Daymion cocked his gun. He walked up behind Kaprice and put the tip to the back of her head. The nigga still had his eyes closed as if he was lost in ecstasy but he opened them as soon as he heard Day's voice.

"Now go on and slide off that shit real nice and slow."

"Oh my God, Daymion. Is that you?"

Kaprice recognized his voice instantly. She couldn't believe that he had walked up on her riding another nigga's dick. For some reason, she was so ashamed of herself, even though, Day was not her man.

"Now you know it's me, but you don't need to worry about all that. I knew your ass couldn't be trusted. That's why I choked your ass with this dick. Bitch, you done slept with my enemy and now you slidin' with his right hand. Did you really believe you could pull me too? You's a grimy ass hoe."

Daymion knew who Big Gun was and could tell that his words cut through Kaprice like a razor to the wrist, but she had made her own choices so who was he to judge her? Gun looked at Day through bloodshot eyes and talked shit that he would soon regret.

"Fuck is wrong with you nigga? Get your lame ass outta here. Don't neither one of us owe you shit."

"Fuck you think you talking nigga? I'll burn this shit down with your naked ass up in it. You betta check that mufuckin' mouth bitch."

Daymion hit Gun with the butt of the weapon and caused a gash to open on the side of his forehead. Some of the blood sprayed in Kaprice's face and on to her naked torso. The nigga went down quickly and when he did, Day kicked him his nut sack and caused him to cry in pain.

"Anything else you want to say to me, bruh? Betta stay the fuck in your place if you want this shit to end in your favor. Bitch ass mufucka."

He looked over at Kaprice and felt disgusted, to think that she had ever had his dick in her mouth made him sick on his stomach. He wanted nothing more than to beat her ass at that very moment. There was nothing he hated more than a disrespectful mufucka. A disloyal bitch had no spot on his team.

"Tie his black ass up and don't try no slick shit."

Kaprice looked as if she was scared to move but when Daymion threw the zip ties down beside her, she quickly jumped up in fear and crawled over to Big Gun.

"Daymion, please don't make me do this. I'm sorry. I didn't mean …"

"Bitch, shut up and do what the hell I told you to do. And make sure you put them mufuckas on tight."

She moved as slow as she could to do what he had told her. She hoped that after she put the ties on Gun's wrists that Day would let her go. She didn't want to be an accomplice to anything he had planned, but he was giving her no choice. She figured that if she got caught up in his bullshit, she'd tell the police everything and even testify if she had to. After she secured the ties like he told her, she looked up at Day and stood. She reached to grab her clothes so she could get dressed and hopefully leave but Day had other plans.

"Nah, what you reaching for? You ain't gonna need none of that. Your ass was so quick to take that shit off so now, you can keep it off."

"Daymion please, just let me get dressed and I'll get out of your way. I won't say anything to anybody. I give you my word."

"Yeah? Well, your word tastes like shit in my mouth. You think I believe anything you tell me? You can't possibly be that dumb. I can't let you walk up outta here and believe that you ain't gonna say shit. Now, take this bag and fill it with all the money he has stashed here and don't act like you don't know where it is."

"You don't have to do this. I got money stashed. You know that and you can have it all."

"Oh, don't worry your pretty little face off. I'll be going to pick that up too. Now, start filling the bag."

Big Gun tried to sit up from the position he was in but the zip ties around his wrist made it hard for him to do. He couldn't believe that he had got caught slipping like that. He wondered if it was his karma for doing Dory dirty. His old friend had kept his pockets laced for years and all because Dory had done one side deal without him, he fucked his bitch as payback. He should have known that it would come back on him. He just didn't expect it so soon. He couldn't even make amends with him because when he went over there to make things right, he had found him slumped over in his wheelchair with a bullet hole in his forehead. Gun didn't even have the decency to call someone to come get his body so he could have a proper burial but instead, he walked out and left him stinking. He didn't know how he was going to do it but he wanted to try and talk Daymion out of killing him. Fuck the bitch. She could be replaced but his life couldn't.

"Aye, aye bruh. This shit here ain't even necessary. Come on and take these things off of me and let's work something out."

"Nah pussy boy. Ain't a fuck thing for us to work out as long as Malachi's money is up in this bitch. Fuck nigga owes me and I'm a keep collecting until I'm paid off."

"Come on. I could help you out. I 'ont like that mufucka anyway. Bitch be stepping on his dope and shit. We could work together and take all his money. Find us a new connect and all. Matter of fact, I know a nigga who could hook us right up. What you say about that? You down with me or not?"

"Nigga, why don't you just shut the fuck up and let me finish what I came here to do and then, I'll be out of your way."

Kaprice had walked back into the living room and passed Daymion the duffel bag. He took it from her and sat it on the table in front of him so he could finish with what he'd had planned. He hated that his life had come to this but it was the only way he knew to bring Malachi out of hiding. Day wasn't trying to get caught and go back to prison so he knew he couldn't hit Malachi while he was out in public. He looked at Kaprice and then at Gun and decided that he would kill the man first. He aimed the gun and without any hesitation, let off a shot. Gun's skull split open immediately and when Kaprice screamed, he knew that she had never witnessed anything like that before.

"Daymion, you didn't have to kill him. You got what you came here for so why are you doing this?"

He turned toward her and aimed the barrel of the gun at her throat. He had thought about letting her suck his dick one more time before he put her out of her misery but he knew she wouldn't bring him any pleasure. Her naked body was perfect and yet, he wasn't turned on at all.

"Oh don't worry, Kaprice, you about to join him. You should have just followed the code. You been dealing with street niggas for a long time so you know the rules. Too bad your ass didn't follow them. Bye bitch, see you in hell."

The bullet left the gun and penetrated her skin just as she was about to speak again. Her words became lost and drowned in the blood that oozed from the wound. He watched her fall back and land on the couch behind her, and he had to admit that she was just as beautiful in death as she was in life. He still couldn't believe that he had almost made plans with a snake that had slithered into his life but he was glad that her true colors had shown before he got caught up.

Day picked up the bag that was full of money and looped the handle around his arm. He pulled out a small bottle of lighter fluid and squirted the contents on their naked bodies and the curtains. He made sure to leave enough so that he could make a trail to the door. He felt no remorse when he turned around and lit the match. He dropped it on to the liquid and it immediately turned into flames and then he ran to his vehicle so that he could flee the scene.

He went back to the room that he shared with Shay and walked inside to find her sleeping. He had thought about letting her stay asleep but he was ready to get out of there so he nudged her shoulder just enough to wake her from her slumber.

"Get up and pack up all our shit. We moving to a place across town and hurry up because I got other shit I need to do."

Shay opened her eyes and slowly sat up in the bed. She didn't even have to wonder where he had been because she already knew.

"You hit another one, didn't you?"

"Don't worry about what I've done. Just get up and get our shit together so we can get out of here."

"Dammit, I told you that I would help you get to him so you don't have to keep taking chances like that. Why don't you stop and just leave his house's alone?"

"When the fuck did you start caring about his houses? Shit, you should be helping me hit those mufuckas. What's up with that anyway?"

"Fuck you, Day. I don't give a damn about him or his houses. I'm just afraid that you are going to run into the wrong one and something bad will happen. Dre needs you and yet, you're out there taking chances with your life, even though you don't have to."

"You just get the shit together like I told you and let me worry about myself unless of course you are trying to protect your dear old dad."

Shay couldnt' believe that he had said that to her but she took it in stride. She had only just met Malachi and hadn't even had time to form any type of bond with him and honestly, she wasn't trying to. She didn't even know what would come of their relationship. They had went and got the paternity test done and as soon as Malachi heard the results he was ecstatic and started to make plans for them. She would like to have thought that knowing he had a daughter would change him but she refused to get her hopes up. She almost felt guilty but that guilt quickly disappeared.

"I'm not moving across town with you. I've been waiting for you to get back so I could tell you that Malachi is getting me a place closer to him. He said that he wants to make up for lost time."

"So, what the fuck does that mean? What are you trying to say here?"

"I think that it's a good idea for me to be closer to him. It will make him trust me more and it will also make it easier for you to get to him."

"Oh yeah, daddy dearest suddenly has a fuckin heart because of you? Bitch ass wanna step up and spend that gwop on you and you just gonna accept it all like you don't know what kind of man he is? You only setting yourself up, unless of course you just don't give a damn."

"Look, I'm just trying to help you, Day, but I don't have to. You can either trust me or not but I need to know which one it's going to be."

Day looked at her sideways because he really wasn't sure if he could trust her no matter how much she claimed to care about Dre. He was finding it hard to believe that she would allow Malachi in so easily. How dare her accept shit the bastard had to give. He looked in Shay's eyes and wasn't sure if he could read deceit or not so he weighed his options.

"Ya know what? I don't need you to help me get to that mufucka. I can get him myself but I will tell you this, if I find out you have anything to do with saving him, I will kill you. I got enough disloyal people in my life and I just don't have room for anymore. Remember that it was your choice to go and I can't save you after that."

"Don't worry Day, you won't have to."

She gathered her belongings and turned to walk out. She hated to do things that way but what other option did she have. She had vowed to pay Malachi back for all the things he had done, especially for the way he had done Dre. She didn't need Daymion Myers to trust her because she would show him who team she was on in due time. She wasn't sure how many other houses he would hit before Malachi caught up with him. She would do everything in her power to save him and then wondered if she would do the same for Malachi.

Day was pissed that Shay had fell for Malachi's bullshit but wasn't a damn thing he could do about it. He was going to eliminate Malachi Jensen one way or the other and not even Shay could stand in his way. He worried about how Dre would feel about Shay's betrayal. He hated knowing that his son could possibly have to suffer more heartbreak. He was too young to have went through so much and wanted nothing more than to protect him.

Since Day wasn't sure of what Shay had really planned, he decided to relocate to a different hotel instead of going to the condo he was going to set them up in. Although, he hadn't told her the exact location he still thought it was best. He gathered his things and walked out to his car and as soon as he got in, his phone rang. When he saw that it was Branch, he answered the call immediately.

"Sup bruh, you ready to make some moves or not?"

"My nigga I don't know what's going on but it seems like a mufucka been getting to that shit before us. Shit up in flames as we speak."

"Nah? Any idea who keeps doing that shit?"

"Not a clue but we need to stop the mufucka because they stepping on our toes and I don't know about you but I feel like putting on my steel toes and going off in they ass. You with me on that?"

"Yeah, you know I'm always down with that."

"Aight, well first we need to get to the next one so let's meet up and do that shit."

Day was tired as fuck but he was not about to pass up an opportunity to hit another one of Malachi's houses and it would also give him a chance to confront Branch on his bullshit. He dared him to deny anything. He would meet up with him and they would go into the house together but only one of them would come back out and if he had his way, it damn sure wouldn't be Branch.

Chapter 13

Dre sat back in the chair and watched the television screen with wide eyes. He watched as the officers pulled Tyre Nichols out of his car and began beating him. The scene was a hard one to watch and it brought tears to his eyes. What shocked him even more was that all five police officers were black men. He wondered what had happened to being your brother's keeper. The cops had been fired and had just been charged with murder. A jury would have to decide their fate but he wondered if the hood would decide it for them first.

The entire city of Memphis, Tennessee was protesting along with New York and other cities across the globe. He could have just as easily been that black man or even his father. He knew that he had played tough when Day questioned him about Malachi, but he never wanted to be looked at as a snitch ass mufucka. He could lay down and do his time no matter how much it was, when he turned twenty one, he would be free again and that is when he would wreak havoc on the blocks. Kenny would be his first victim. That pussy ass mufucka was too soft to be his friend and Dre was pissed that he didn't pick up on that shit sooner. Kenny didn't have to be jealous of Dre because he had looked at him as his equal and never would have left him behind.

He was so engrossed in the story on the screen that he didn't see the two boys walk up on him until it was too late. The boys were older and bigger than him but Dre was a

Myers and his heart didn't pump Kool -aid. As a matter of fact, it didn't pump anything at all because it had died long ago.

"Get your punk ass up. That's my seat you sitting in."

"Yeah bitch, get the hell up."

Dre ignored the two boys and continued to watch the story he had been listening to. A mufucka didn't tell him what to do. He moved and acted on his own accord and he'd be damned if he let someone else change that. When the boys noticed that he wasn't getting up, they got in front of him and blocked his view.

"Did you hear what the fuck I just said? Nigga, you need to get the hell outta my seat. My show about to come on and you in my way."

Dre looked up at the boy and smiled an evil smile. True enough, Dre was shorter but he had big courage and refused to bow down.

"Yeah, I heard you bitch but I ain't moving until I'm ready. You don't own shit but you can have it as soon as the news goes off. But until then, I'd appreciate it if you get the fuck from in front of me so I can finish watching this."

"Nah, lil nigga, who the hell you think you talking to?"

"I'm talking to you and your pussy ass potna. The fuck you gonna do about it?"

The two boys reached out and grabbed Dre by the shirt and pulled him out of the chair. He landed on the floor with a loud thud with the concrete scraping his elbow. He felt the boys pound into him and tried as hard as he could to block their blows. He couldn't lie, every time their fists made contact, that shit hurt. Dre refused to let them know it, though. He thought about Tyre Nichols and how he had felt when those cops beat him. His heart broke for a man he had never met but thinking of him gave Dre a new found strength.

He thought about the night that Malachi had beat him for selling someone else's drugs. His whole body had been in pain but he had found the will to get up and keep moving. The longer he thought about it, the less the blows hurt. He decided that he would fight back, not only for himself but for Tyre Nichols too. He began to kick and punch with all of his might until the two boys landed on their backs. He got up and stood over them while his sweat dripped on their bodies.

"Now niggas, like I said, when I'm done watching the news I'll get up and not a minute before."

Dre turned and sat back down in the chair that he had been pulled from and turned the television up. The boys finally got up off the floor embarrassed by what had happened. They had to admit that Dre was a different breed than other boys in the center, and they would never fuck with him again. They were glad that no one else had been in the TV room to witness what had happened. As long as no one else knew, then they wouldn't talk about it.

After the news went off, Dre got up and went to his room. He passed the two boys who had tried to bully him out of the television and neither of them looked his way. He was going to tell them that he was done and it was all theirs but changed his mind. They could figure that shit out themselves.

Dre had a lot of time to do and it would give him plenty of time to think about the moves he would make once he hit the streets again. He lied in his bed in the silence and fell asleep without a care in the world. He woke up the next morning to the staff calling him for a visit. His father hadn't mentioned coming back so he wondered who it could be. He got dressed and made his way to the visiting room and was shocked by who was there.

"Hey Dre, I hope you're doing okay in here. I talked my grandma into bringing me to see you. She wanted to see you too. So, here we are."

About that time, Miss Dot appeared with an arm full of drinks and snacks. He couldn't believe that her and Tasha had come to see him but he was so glad that they did. He had really missed them.

"Come on son, help Miss Dot with some of this food. You see me struggling here."

Dre laughed and grabbed some of the snacks and then sat at the table to enjoy his visit. He wondered where Kenny's coward ass was at so he asked.

"Aye Tasha, thanks for coming to see me but where is your brother?"

"I don't know, Dre. Me and grandma haven't seen him since the night they took you away. He packed a few of his things and dipped. We don't know where he's at."

"Well son, I think my grandson was ashamed of how he did you. I've tried to raise him and Natasha right but I can only do so much."

"It's okay, Miss Dot. You did the best you could do."

Tasha smiled and scooted her chair a little closer to his. Time apart had not changed her feelings for him. She had promised him that she would always be his rider and she meant it with all her heart. They sat and enjoyed the time they had together until the guard came over and informed Dre that someone else was there to see him and was on their way inside. Tasha thought that she was finally going to meet the infamous Daymion Myers but when the visitor walked in , her whole demeanor changed.

"What the hell is she doing here?"

Dre could not believe his eyes. Shay was still as pretty as the day he had first met her and it caused his body to break out in chills. He could hear Tasha smack her lips and talk shit but nothing could change how he felt at that moment.

"Hey Dre, I'm sorry it took me so long to show up. I hope you'll forgive me. We have so much to catch up on, so I hope you don't mind me showing up like this."

Tasha was pissed because she couldn't stand Shay. She knew that Dre had a thing for her but Shay was older than him so she didn't think that it would ever work between them. She believed that one day, Dre would wake up and see that she was the only girl for him.

"Don't you see that he already has visitors. You a rude ass bitch and I think you should go."

"Natasha, how dare you be disrespectful like that? I raised you better. Now, we have been here for a couple of hours, so let's go and allow someone else to have some time with him."

Tasha couldn't believe that her grandmother was willing to leave and let Shay visit with Dre. Her grandmother had to have known how that would make her feel, but she obviously didn't care. She didn't want to leave Dre with her competition but she didn't have much of a choice.

"Sorry grandma but she doesn't deserve to be with him. I think she should be the one to leave."

"Nope, now let's get out of here. We'll see you again soon, son. Take care of yourself."

Miss Dot grabbed Tasha's arm and led her out of the visiting room against her will. She was sick on her stomach thinking about what Dre and Shay would talk about. They didn't belong together and one day, Dre would realize that and come running to her, but she decided that he shouldn't wait too long because it could very well be too late. She wondered what Dre's father would think about his son being in love.

Meanwhile, Dre was in dreamland. He couldn't believe that Shay was right in front of him. He had thought that he would never see her again. Just her presence had made everything so much better. She said that she had some important things to talk to him about and he wondered just what they were.

"Dre, I have something that I need to tell you. Something that I should have told you before. I just hope that it doesn't change things between us."

"Come on Shay, I might be younger than you but I'm just as mature. You know that you can tell me anything."

Shay bit her bottom lip, a nervous habit she had inherited from her mother, and also one that she hated. "Dre, I want you to know that I kept this from you for your own good, and I just think that it's something you should be aware of. If you don't want to fool with me anymore after you hear this I will understand."

"Well, what are you waiting for? Just spit it out."

"Okay. Remember I told you that I wanted to one day meet my father and tell him that I was his daughter."

"Yeah. Did you find out who he was?"

"Yeah Dre, but I've known all along who my father was. I just didn't tell you or anyone else who he was."

"Okay. So who is your father, Shay?"

"Malachi Jensen."

Dre could not believe his ears. How dare her keep something like that from him? He had a right to know. He felt sick on his stomach to think that he dreamed to one day be with the enemy's daughter. What would his father say about something like that?

"How you Malachi's daughter? That don't even make sense, Shay."

"It's true, Dre. My mother had me so young but she made Malachi believe that I died. She wanted to keep me safe from him and his clutches. She wanted me to have a better life so she sent me to live with my uncle. Teddy was my cousin Dre, not my brother. I guess that I was too ashamed to tell anyone, but now Malachi knows and so does your father."

"My dad knows? How? And what you got to do with my dad?"

"I met your father one day when I went to Dory's. He had went there looking for you but you were already in Malachi's grip. I told him who I was and who you were to me. I vowed to help him find you but you were found a little too late. When I told him that Malachi was my father, he was pissed until I told him that I would help him get to him but your father is an impatient man."

"So you telling me that you been out there chilling with my dad and he ain't say shit to me about it."

"Don't be mad at him, Dre. He wanted to make sure that you really meant something to me before he told you. He said that he was tired of people hurting you and wasn't about to let me do it. He was only looking out for your best interest."

"So, why you here now? My dad know you here?"

"No Dre, he doesn't. You dad doesn't agree with Malachi putting me up in a place to live and acting like a real father to me but it's all a part of my plan. I need Malachi to trust me so that I can set him up for Daymion, but he doesn't believe me. He thinks that I'll fall weak for Malachi's gestures and turn on you and him."

"So, what you want me to do?"

"I want you to convince your father that I am not the enemy. I only want to help him get to Malachi."

"So, you saying you gonna set your own father up and hand him over to mine? Where exactly is your loyalty at Shay? Are you setting up Malachi or are you setting up my dad? I need to know the truth."

She didn't answer him right away and to him that said everything. Dre was young but he had the mind of a grown man. He was wise beyond his years and more mature than most people twice his age. He could tell from the look in her eyes that she wasn't sure whose side she was on and he didn't have time for someone else in his life whom he wasn't sure he could trust.

"It's all good, Shay. You don't have to answer that because you already have. Thanks for coming to see me but please, don't ever come back."

Dre stood and motioned his arm for the guard to come get him and take him back to his room. He had mad love for Shay but at the end of the day, love meant nothing if there was no loyalty. Shay couldn't be loyal to her father and to his. They were enemies and she would have to choose. Dre knew what side she would pick and he couldn't take the chance of her betraying him so he let her go. He felt like one day they would be at war and he needed to be able to defend his side. He couldn't do that if he held a soft spot for her. He decided that one more let down wouldn't kill him. He would just have to learn to move on. His father would be proud and he couldn't wait to tell him.

Shay left the juvenile center with a heavy heart. She couldn't believe that Dre had walked out and told her to never come back. She had real love for him but he was right. She couldn't play both sides so she would have to choose one. She wasn't sure if she would choose the right one in the end. She hoped that by the time Dre got out, he would have a change of heart but that was still a ways off.

Her father had no clue that she felt for Dre and he also didn't know that she knew of his evil deeds against Dre. She wondered just how he would react if he found out. Would he spare her because she was his seed or would he not forgive her for her disloyalty? She would wait until they got closer and then she would tell him, she just hoped that it wouldn't be too late for her and Dre but it was a chance she would be willing to take to make things right between them.

Chapter 14

"Sup bruh, you ready to do this shit?"

"Hell yeah nigga. I been waiting on you to say the word with your slow moving ass. Shit, I was starting to feel like you was getting scared to pull it off."

"Nah, a nigga like me ain't scared of shit. We 'bout to get laced the fuck up and my dick is hard just thinking about it."

"Yeah B, I know just what you saying. I'm ready so let's do this."

Branch had no idea that Day knew about the other side he was playing on, but by the end of the night he would be exposed for who he really was, whoever that may be. Branch also had no clue that it was Day himself who had hit the other two houses but he planned on letting him know that too. Branch had turned out to be a snake ass mufucka and Day didn't deal with people like that so he had to get rid of him.

He thought about Mellow, who still sat behind enemy lines. He had only met him while doing his last year in prison but he seemed to be a real ass nigga. Day had kept his word and stayed in contact with him. He made sure he kept his commissary account full and sent him anything else he needed to survive.

He would continue to stack paper and rebuild his empire until Mellow was released. Together, they would take over the hood and do shit their way. Mellow seemed thorough enough and on top of that, it was him who told Day about what was going on with Dre in the streets.

Mellow had never really liked Dory and it was his dawg, Teddy who had hooked them up. Mellow didn't get down with a lot of the shit that Dory's crew did but his pockets did stay laced so he never complained.

When Mellow met Daymion Myers, they clicked instantly and the rest was history. Mellow was just as stoked about working with Day as he was with him.

Branch insisted on Day driving and he wasn't about to complain. Day figured that it would make it easier for him to get away if he already had the keys in his possession. The blacked out Denali easily fit in with the other vehicles that were parked in the neighborhood so it wouldn't stand out. Branch had brought the gloves and masks and even the artillery. Day had told him that he didn't have anything to work with, which was a lie that had been necessary. Day felt like if he would have told him that he already had his own supplies, Branch may have put two together and figured out that he had already been in action. That was the last thing he needed so he played it as safe as he could.

"Yo, Day, we gonna hit two of these mufuckas tonight and get all that we can get. Malachi and his crew ain't gon' have shit when we get through. I can't wait to shut that shit down. How 'bout you, bruh? You feeling good about this jack? Bitches ain't even gonna expect it."

"Damn right I'm feeling good. Can't wait to run up in that bitch and handle them mufuckas. Now I know you did your homework so what we looking at?"

"Aight so it's three niggas up in that bitch. Two males and a ho that wished she had a dick but I'm a set that ho straight and kick her dead in the pussy."

"Nigga, you wild as fuck, but let's get ready so we can do this. We can't sit here all night and talk. Shit ain't gonna get done like that. What are we waiting on?"

"Bet that. Let's put this gear on and do what we do best."

Day and Branch slid on their gloves and black masks. When Branch handed him the gun, it felt like it belonged in his hand. He had always loved the feel of cold steel even with the gloves on. Day wasn't worried about what was going down because after he'd hit the first two houses his adrenaline had spiked. He hated having a co-defendant but doing the hit with Branch was necessary. He felt like it was the best way to take his ass out.

"Aight bruh, I'm gonna cover the front of the house and you go through the back. These mufuckas always be on some gambling shit so they probably at the card table as we speak. Ain't nothing sweeter than catching a man off guard and taking his shit over."

"Yeah, but we still need to be careful. I ain't trying to die in there. I got a son I need to be there for. Know what I'm saying?"

"Yeah Day, a nigga feels where you coming from and don't worry, you gon' make it back to ya boy in one piece."

They gave each other dap and exited the ride carefully. It was late and very few fiends were out but they were so high that they wouldn't have noticed them even if they walked right past them. Once Day and Branch unlatched the front gate, they slid into the yard. Day crept to the back of the house like Branch had told him to and Branch walked up on the front porch. Day peeked through the windows on his way to the back and saw that the trio were at a table with cards in their hands just like Branch had said. It made him feel like Branch had been there before instead of hearing about their gambling from rumors. The trio looked a little too comfortable to him making it seem like something was off but Day had hoped that he was just being paranoid.

He decided to go with his first mind and turn around. He felt like if he walked through that back door it would end up bad for him. He would wait for Branch to go in and follow behind him. Day was a smart nigga and Trey had always told him the signs to look for when you thought a mufucka was trying to deceive you.

He noticed that Branch had already disappeared inside and quietly made his way behind him. He didn't hear any type of commotion so either all three of the niggas around the card table were cooperating or dead unless his mind had led him right. He peeked around the corner and saw Branch standing over the three of them at the table but no one seemed to be afraid of what was about to go down. Day nodded his head because he had been right. The jack was a setup. One that he had already predicted but little did they know, there had been a change in plans.

Day quietly sat down the gun that Branch had given him because he didn't think that the gun would be useful anyway. He had come prepared, though. He pulled a semi out of the waist of his jeans and held it tightly in his hand. A mufucka would pay for their disloyalty because it was a trait that he wasn't fond of in people. He peeked around the corner again and saw Branch walk to the back door. As soon as he put his hand on the doorknob, Day walked in to view and threw everyone off guard.

"You looking for someone, playa?"

Branch turned around, his weapon by his side relaxed. Not a normal move for a nigga about to jack somebody.

"Damn bruh, what took you so long to get in here? I thought you was coming in from the back."

"Nah, I ain't think that was a good move. I'm trying to figure out why it was one you chose for me to make. Look like you pretty relaxed in this bitch to me. What's up with that shit?"

One of the three at the table made a quick move but Day made one quicker. The bullets ripped through all three of them only because he didn't know which one was about to try him. They didn't stand a chance against Day, and Branch wouldn't stand one either.

"Aye man, chill with that shit. You done killed all three of them, so how we pose to know where the shit at?"

"Something tell me you already know so why don't you go ahead and lead me to it before you look like them."

"Nigga, what you getting at? The fuck you trying to say?"

"Come on B, you be trying to make it like me and you is in tune with each other but bitch I ain't never betrayed a mufucka I'm 'pose to be cool with. I ain't a fucking snake like you. Now lead me to that stash. Matter of fact, go head and drop that piece in your hand because you ain't gonna need it no more."

Day could see his trigger finger twitch but he refused to give him a chance to use it so he pulled back on his semi and fired. The gun flew out of Branch's hand so quick he couldn't have stopped it if he'd tried. Day was a perfect shot because Trey started training him at a young age and when Trey was killed, Day went to the city dump and set up targets to let out his frustration hitting everyone on point. Niggas use to pick on his city dump training but Day wasn't bothered by it. That was the only place that was open and far enough away so that no one would bother him. He also didn't have to worry about the local police bothering him.

"Nigga, why you tripping? I'm on your side of this shit. I thought we was cool. We made plans to take all this shit over. Don't you remember that bruh?"

"Nah mufucka, let me tell you what I do remember. You was 'pose to get out here and look for my seed and take care of him but once you bounced, you forgot about all of that. You never had any intentions on finding Dre, but even when you ran into him you ain't did shit for him."

"What the fuck you talking about, Day? Nigga you losing me right now. I ain't never met that boy. You got shit confused."

"Confused? Nah nigga, you the one that got shit confused when you thought you was gonna lead me in blind to a setup, bitch. I know all about you giving my son that shit to sell and when Malachi caught him with it you stood by and allowed that mufucka to beat my boy. Then, your black ass gave him a gun and told him to kill Malachi but he shot the wrong man and now, he sitting behind those fucking walls until his twenty first birthday. What happened to your loyalty?"

"See, now you really don't know what you saying. I 'ont even fuck with Malachi. I ain't neva even been around his grimy ass."

"You ain't gotta lie no more Branch or should I call you Tree? Yeah, I know that too. I saw your ass the other night sitting in that restaurant with the enemy and bitch ass Kiara. You gonna deny that too?"

Branch couldn't even deny what he'd been accused of because it was the truth. He'd been found out and wasn't shit he could do about it.

"So, what now Day? You gon' kill me too? Huh? Shit, you can't blame me for trying to come up and make a way for myself. That street shit was given to you by a nigga who knew how to handle it, but me, man I ain't neva had a mufucka care enough about me to teach me shit. All that talk in prison from those niggas who looked up to you but you ain't that same nigga to me. You ain't a fucking king to me, bruh. You just another mufucka who has others doing shit for you. Your ass don't know nothing about putting in work. Nigga you ain't even gotta work for pussy. Them bitches throw that shit to you but I got to take it from a ho. You wasn't gonna ever share the spotlight with me and I'd be damned if I walked in your shadow so go head and do what you need to do."

"See B, you wrong. You were like a long lost brother to me and I would have never put you behind me. You would have never been a shadow because you shined too bright. We would have walked the same walk because I saw you as an equal. You was my nigga and it kills me to have to do this but I got to because once you betray me and I forgive you. That's an open invitation for you to do it to me again. That's why betrayal and disloyalty are forbidden. You brought all of this on yourself."

Day raised the gun but before he had a chance to pull the trigger, Branch tried one more thing to stall him.

"Hold up. Don't you need me to show you where that shit at? You gonna walk outta this bitch empty handed if you kill me first so you better think about that."

"Hmm, yeah, I did think about that but then I remembered that you ain't that good of a leader. Thanks, but I already know where to go. Your services are no longer needed. Rest in misery, mufucka."

The bullets came out and sprayed Branch's body knocking him backwards. Day watched but felt no remorse, hell he didn't have any left. He had got so close to him while they were locked up and never could have guessed that things would turn out the way they did. He was truly disappointed in the man that was on the floor dead from his hands, but shit had to keep moving. Day stuffed the semi in the back of his pants and went to the laundry room where he pulled the fake washing machine from the wall. The money and drugs stuffed inside the back of it already bagged up and ready to go. Day was sure that Branch and the three workers had set it up to be easy to grab for themselves. He just wondered which ones would be left behind for Malachi to find.

He left the laundry room and stole one last glance at Branch and his other victims before he left the house. The fiends that had been outside were long gone and others living close had been asleep for hours. The sounds of gun shots were the norm so no one woke up anymore to investigate because the police didn't give a fuck anyway. Most feared

Malachi Jensen more than anything else and knew better than to run their mouth.

He jumped back in the Denali and when he pushed the key into the ignition it purred softly to life. He had planned to continue to stack his rations until he could run the hood without threat. One of his problems had just been taken care of but he had more to go. He had asked Shay to give him the location of where Malachi laid his head at night but she refused. She said that she would bring Malachi to him once she gained his trust. She felt like things were safer that way but Day thought she was full of shit too. He wasn't beyond killing her too, because Dre could find love with another.

He drove the Denali to the same city dump he had used for target practice and lit it on fire. He made sure to drop the product and cash off first and then he walked back to it. He had to admit he was tired so he went to the hotel he had moved to after Shay left and as soon as his head hit the pillow, he was out.

The knock on the door woke him the next morning, but when he realized it was room service he turned them away and asked them to come back later. He took his time getting dressed for whatever that night would bring and once he finally stepped back out, everything he had wished for fell right in his lap.

He watched as she walked into the store and grabbed a shopping cart. She was thick and curvy and even better than he had remembered. He walked in behind her and followed at a safe distance watching her every move. Her hips swayed with the ease of a super model and caused his dick to react but it was too bad he couldn't act on that reaction. She walked down almost every aisle and took her time without a care in the world. However, she didn't know that a predator was lurking and she would be the prey.

When she was done filling her cart, she drove her purchases to the checkout counter but he never once lost sight. He chose the counter behind her and paid for the couple of things he had picked up and then walked out ahead of her. He stood by the pay phone and waited until she walked to her car and once again he followed. Once she opened her back door and went to put the bags in the back seat that was when he made his move.

"You look like you need some help there."

She smiled at the voice without looking up but when she finally lifted her head she saw the last person she wanted to see.

"Oh, my God. Daymion."

"Hello Kiara, I'm back bitch and you already know what that means."

Chapter 15

Malachi had a strange feeling in his gut and he tried to ignore it but it just wouldn't go away. He looked at his diamond encrusted Rolex and noticed the time. Kiara had never been late when he allowed her to go out by herself, which wasn't very often. He had got the call that another house had been hit and all four workers had been taken out. He was vexed by that because there had only been three workers assigned to that location. He had asked Shay to go and check things out for him and when she called and reported that Tree had been at the house also. He knew that it had been a set up but he didn't know by who.

He knew that he had been wrong to send his daughter out to the block to see what was going on but he felt like even she had to earn her place. He had to know that he could trust her or she would have to be eliminated because no one rode beside him if he couldn't trust them. He heard the front door and hoped that it was Kiara but it was Shay instead.

It wasn't that he missed Kiara but she was his property and until he felt like he was tired of her he wanted to keep her. She was a good fuck and could suck the hell out of his dick. He knew that he could find that anywhere but he liked it within reach whenever he wanted it. He would kill her if he found out she was giving his pussy away without his permission. When he found out that Cardo had been in the bed with her when he was shot, he was pissed at the betrayal. He had allowed Cardo to fuck Kiara but only when he wanted to watch her perform. They knew not to do it when he wasn't around. Cardo should have listened because a piece of pussy had cost him his life.

"The scene was a mess but I called your crew to go and clean it up."

"Did it look like my three workers had tried to defend themselves?"

"No Malachi, it actually looked like there may have been someone else in the house. To be honest, I think Tree went in with someone else to jack your crew and whoever it was turned on him. Not one of your workers even had a weapon close to them so I don't know. I think they were caught off guard."

"Yeah that or either they were down with a plan that had been changed at the last minute."

"So, what now?"

"It's time to get the hell out of dodge and lay low for a while. Somebody is coming for me and I feel like they are getting really damn close."

"My mother made it seem like you were so brave so why would you run? What about me, Malachi. We just found each other and you ready to bail so soon?"

He looked up at her and thoughts of Malia came to him. He would give anything to have Malaia back but there he was with a daughter who was her spitting image. He hadn't seen it at first but as the days went by, he could see it more and more, and yet he had sent that piece of her out into the danger zone. He had lost Malia at the hands of the enemy but he vowed to do all he could to protect Shay. That was what Malia would have expected of him even though she had kept her from him.

"I am brave Shay, but I got someone else to worry about now. I have to protect you or risk losing you the same way I lost your mother."

"How are you going to protect me if you run from what's chasing you? Without you, it gives them more power to reach me. Are you really going to let that happen?"

"No, I'm not and that's why I'm taking you with me. I got to get you out of here at least until I find out who is coming at me and I can get rid of them. I won't leave you behind."

"So what if I don't want to go? This place is all I know and I'm not ready to change that."

"I'm not giving you a choice. You come willingly or I force you. Doesn't matter to me but you ain't staying here. Besides, there's nothing here for you to stay for, unless of course, you're not telling me something."

"What are you implying?"

"Nothing. That's why you're leaving with me. No, I won't tell you again. All you have can be left behind. We'll start over."

"What? There are things that are sentimental to me and I need to go get them."

"Everything is replaceable, even people. I'll send a worker to get what's important to you but you're not going back to your place. For all we know, it could be next. We'll be leaving within the hour so you might as well be ready. I have a few calls to make and then I'll send for us a car."

Malachi walked out of the room and left Shay dumbfounded. The last thing she wanted to do was leave town with him and not be able to tell anyone where she was. She thought about Dre and the disappointed look that she had left him with. She felt like she would one day win him back but if she left, he would never forgive her.

Shay had thought about picking up her phone and giving Day a call but she was too afraid that Malachi would walk in and catch her. He would want to know who she was talking to and she would have no explanation. She hadn't mentioned any friends or associates so he would definitely be on guard. She decided that she would just go with the flow and give him a call once they got to their destination, wherever that might have been.

When Malachi walked back into the room, he carried a black cloth in his hand and walked up behind her. Before she even realized he was there he put the cloth over her nose and held it there until she fell back in his arms. He had only just met her so he knew that he couldn't be too careful. He figured that if she didn't know where they were at then there was no way she could give anyone else the information. It was just a precaution because he couldn't afford to take any chances.

"Yo Bones, come in here and carry my daughter out to the ride, and be careful with her. She's still fragile."

"Yes sir boss, but can I ask why you put her out like that?"

"No, you can't. I don't pay you to ask me questions about my movements. Now, do what I said or I can hire someone who will."

Bones turned without saying another word and picked Shay up carefully in his arms as if she were only a baby. Malachi had done many things that he didn't understand but that was the first time he had questioned it. He thought that Malachi finding out he had a daughter would change something inside of him but he had been wrong. Bones had been working for him since he was a teenager and had at first, looked up to the man but over time he saw Malachi's true colors. However, it was too late to pull out. Bones had always believed in loyalty, even to a mufucka that didn't deserve it.

After he carried Shay out and put her in the front passenger seat, he put on her seatbelt and pulled the lever back so the seat would lay down. He wondered how Malachi had made such a beautiful daughter but then he remembered the old photos he had found lying around one day and got his answer. Shay had definitely taken after her mother who had been a beauty herself. He stared at her until he heard Malachi walk up behind him.

"You can stare all you want but you better not ever try her. You have been here long enough to know my rules. Kiara was one thing but my daughter is completely off limits."

"Sorry boss, I don't mean any disrespect. I just couldn't help myself."

"Oh yeah? That's what the last nigga I murked said right before I shot him between the eyes. It may never be intentional but it's still the same thing. Always remember that."

Malachi got in and started the vehicle and put it in reverse before Bones backed away and shut Shay's door. He had no idea where Malachi was going because he had never told anyone in his crew about his hideouts. When he left, he always took what was important to him and nothing else and that was the first time he had taken a passenger. Malachi hoped that Shay would forgive him. He was only doing it to protect her and hopefully she would understand.

Malachi had left his underlings to take care of what he had left behind. He always assigned the same people and they had never let him down. He never trusted many people because so many had abandoned him during his life. Malachi had never felt loved so he didn't know how to give it back.

His father was a pimp who got killed only two weeks before he was born and his mother died of cancer when he was only seven years old. He became a ward of the state because no one stepped up to take him. When he was put in a foster home at nine years old, he was molested by the woman's husband almost every night. Malachi was terrified to go home from school every day because he knew what would happen once he lied down every night to go to sleep. He often had to rest his head on his desk in class but when his teacher noticed it, she threatened to go to the principal. He finally decided to leave his school books and school supplies in his dresser and replaced those items in his book bag with a few toiletries and a change of clothes. He had thought about taking some snacks too but he knew that he wouldn't be able to break the lock on the refrigerator. He decided to figure that part out when he got to it.

When he got off the bus at school, he walked the opposite direction and never looked back. He met Shakim Allah known to the streets as Quack and was propositioned with a delivery job. At first, Malachi had no idea what he would be delivering but because he was hungry and had no money, or no place to go, he took the job, and never asked questions. He only found out what he had been carrying when he was busted getting off the Amtrak. Officers pushed him to the ground and opened up the bag he'd had strapped to his back where four kilos of cocaine were stored. He was put in a juvenile camp and sentenced to two years behind the wall. Malachi was a loner and didn't trust anyone enough to even give them a chance. The counselor tried hard to get him to open up but he had nothing to share. When he was released, he went back to Quack and told him that he was ready to get back on his grind.

"You know what kid, I gotta give it to you. I really thought that you was going to sell me out but you surprised me and kept your mouth shut. For that, I'm going to reward you."

Quack purchased a small one bedroom apartment for him to stay in. He figured that Malachi was mature enough to have his own place. He also sent over two of his bottom bitches to teach Malachi everything he needed to know about sex. As the years passed, he grew stronger in the drug game and soon had his own crew and his own empire. Quack wasn't selfish when it came to Malachi because the kid had truly proven himself. He vowed to never hold him back and when he felt the kid was ready, he let him spread his wings and fly.

Not too long after he created his own organization, he met thirteen year old Malia. She was the most beautiful girl he had ever seen and although he was older he knew that he had to have her but she wouldn't be his only one. Malia wasn't experienced in sex like he was so he often had to fuck other women to satisfy his urges. His sexual preferences was often rough and he thought of Malia as too delicate to handle his beast mode, but everything changed when she ended up pregnant.

He had lost all respect for her because she thought it would be best for them to separate so he wouldn't get in trouble for getting her pregnant but instead of being by herself, Malia ran to another boy, one that was closer to her age. Things were never the same between them after that and when Malia was killed, he felt guilty and never forgave himself. Malachi felt like he could make things right by taking care of Shay.

When he pulled into his hide away he heard her as she woke up. She looked around and wondered where he had taken her but he wasn't giving her any clues.

"Where are we, Malachi? How could you do this? How could you ever expect me to trust you if you do stuff like this to me?"

"I'll do whatever I have to do to make sure you don't suffer the same fate as your mother did."

"Nobody is going to hurt me, Malachi. Dammit, it's you they want that's why I came to you. I thought it would be the only way to protect you."

"Wait a minute, what the hell are you saying? You have known that someone was coming for me and you ain't say shit."

"I'm sorry, Malachi. I somehow knew that you'd react his way, but no one is going to get you as long as I'm with you."

"Who is it? Who the fuck has been robbing my spots trying to get to me and you better not lie?"

Shay watched as Malachi pulled out his gun and loaded it. She tried to discreetly feel for her phone but it was gone. She would have no way to call for help if things took another turn. She had no clue where she was at but she had to find out a way to escape him.

"Malachi, please. I have nothing to do with what they have done. I tried to stop him from robbing those houses but he wouldn't listen, but he doesn't know how to find you."

The more Shay talked, the madder Malachi became. He wondered why she had waited to tell him everything. He didn't want to believe that his own daughter had set him up but he had to admit that everything started happening to him when she came into his life. It would break his heart to have to kill her but he wouldn't hesitate if that's what it came to.

"I find it kind of strange that my houses started getting hit when you came along. I don't believe in coincidences so I need to know for sure that you have had nothing to do with all the hits on my posts."

"I don't, Malachi. I would never go along with something like that. I tried to stop him. I saw it in his eyes and I warned him but he refused to listen to me. There was nothing I could do to stop him."

"You keep saying him. Tell me who you keep referring to. I want the truth, so tell me his name. Tell me who I'm going to kill."

Her heartbeat sped up as she looked up into his eyes. She had said too much and spoke too soon. She thought about lying but knew the consequences behind getting caught. She had run out of options. She was given no other choice. She pursed her lips together and gave Malachi what he'd asked for.

"Daymion Myers."

Chapter 16

"Daymion please, I'm sorry that I had you locked up but you gave me no other choice. You acted like I wasn't shit to you anymore. For God's sake I had your son, your first born."

"You lied to me, Kiara. You kept your real age from me and when I found out, I left your ass alone. You couldn't have possibly expected me to stay with you after that, but I would have taken care of my seed and you knew that. You sent me away and then treated my son like dirt on the bottom of your shoes. I can't forgive you for that. You never even brought him to see me. You ain't shit to me but you gonna make that shit up."

"I'll do anything for you and you know that, but can you give us one more chance? Me, you and Dreighton, we can be a family. We can leave everything behind and move out of this place. I'm not a child anymore, Daymion. I can please you just how you like it. I never forgot how good you felt inside of me."

Kiara reached her hand over and placed it on his dick print, but he shot her down before she had a chance to do anything else. Day could not believe that she actually thought he would stick his dick inside of her. Yeah, time had did her body very well and even in Malachi Jensen's clutches, she had not lost her shine. Looking at her brought back memories of when he first met her. She was thick in all the right places and seemed to have a good head on her shoulders. He never could have guessed that she had been only fifteen.

She was mature and even had her own money, although he refused to let her spend it. She belonged to him and his woman didn't have to go in her own purse because he always had one set aside for her. There wasn't a moment that passed that he didn't want to spend with her but when he asked her to move in with him she had an excuse of why she couldn't, but her excuse wasn't good enough. That was when he started digging deeper and found out her real age.

Day cut things off with her immediately and refused to give her a chance to explain. She had jeopardized him and he couldn't understand why. He had jumped back into his old routines after they parted ways only for her to call him a few weeks later and tell him that she was pregnant. He didn't believe her at first and thought that it was just a plot to get him back but when the baby inside of her began to grow, he knew that he was fucked. Day was a man and he vowed to take care of his responsibilities. He would make sure that the baby had everything he needed but he would not be with Kiara.

The day that Dreighton was born, Day had showed up to sign the birth certificate. He didn't want to miss seeing his son come into the world but after the ink had dried, the local authorities showed up and arrested him for sexual battery on a minor. He tried to get Kiara to save him but she refused. He also been caught with drugs, which sealed his fate.

"Kiara, come on, you gonna let them take me away like this? That shit was consensual and you know it. You can't let them take me. Kiara, I'm gonna end up going to prison. Come on and speak up."

"No Daymion, I won't help you unless you agree to marry me. It's already been proven that he is yours so let's get married and be a family."

"Hell no, I would rather rot inside of a prison cell than be stuck with you forever. One day, you'll regret this. Mark my words."

He would never forgive Kiara for all he and his son had went through. She didn't deserve it. Because of her, Dre was where Day had never wanted him to be. Dre should be out living the life a boy his age lived. He should be in school getting an education and planning what he wanted to be when he got older but instead, he was locked away like an animal, but one thing was certain, he was safe and out of the way so that Day could get to Malachi. No one could hurt Dre where he was and that gave him a small sense of relief.

"Where are we going, Daymion?"

"That's the same thing that I was about to ask you. Where are we going?"

"I don't understand. You decided to grab me at the grocery store so you must have had a plan in mind. What are you going to do with me?"

"Well, you're going to tell me where Malachi is at. He's the one I really want Kiara, so if you want to save yourself then that's the only way you can do it."

"I can't take you to him because if I do he will kill me."

"And if you don't, I'll kill you so choose whose hands you'd rather die by. Mine or his."

Kiara had known Day long enough to know that he meant what he said but she also knew that Malachi would not spare her. She was in a no win situation and wondered how she was going to get out of it. She couldn't just sit there though, she knew that she had to try.

"Okay, I'll take you to him but you have to promise me that you will let me go after that. Who's going to be around for Dre if you kill me? You'll go to prison and I'll be dead. Are you really going to leave him on his own like that?"

"Are you really asking me that? My fucking son has been on his own ever since he came out of that rank ass pussy you been passing out to Malachi and his crew. Don't act like you give a damn now. You let me worry about my son because if I have my way, you will never see him again."

"Really, Daymion? You would really cut me out of my child's life? He needs his mother. He needs me and I'll be damned if I let you take him from me."

"Fuck you, Kiara. You have treated my son like shit long enough. You made him go out there in the fucking streets and sell dope in order to eat. You fucked mufuckas in front of him and laughed about that shit like it was nothing, and you never, not once brought him to see me. You know who brought him bitch? Kayla, that's who. I was able to meet my son because of her. She at least had the decency to care about what he wanted most."

"Fuck that white bitch."

"Oh, don't worry Kiara, I did. She ended up being better than you." Daymion told the lie with ease.

"Are you still fucking her Daymion? I knew that bitch wanted you back when we first met. I had to watch that ho because I felt like she would have tried you. It's good to know that I would have been right."

"Well, me or you neither one has to worry about her. So you can stop trying to change the subject."

Day was growing tired of waiting for her to tell him what he wanted to know. He pulled down a side street and parked and got out. He walked around the vehicle and yanked the passenger side door open and pulled her out.

"You think I'm playing with you bitch? Well, I'm not. You fucking owe me for all those years I spent locked up because of you and now I'm ready to collect. Now, you either pay up willingly or by force but you gonna give me what I want. Now you're gonna tell me where the hell I need to go to get to Malachi and I'm not asking anymore, I'm telling you."

"Okay, okay. I'll take you to the house, Daymion. Just let me go get back in the car and I'll tell you."

When her and Day were together he had never raised a hand to her so for him to threaten her that way stunned her. She had never been more scared of anyone in her life, not even Malachi. She would take Day to the house that her and Malachi shared. She knew that Malachi had to be worried she had always come back on time so he would already be on alert. When he realizes that she was with Day, he would be pissed but she would have to worry about that when they got there. She had to make him believe that she was not with Day by choice, and then he would save her and get rid of Day for good.

When Day got back in the ride, she gave him directions and although it was far off the roads of the city, he still found it with ease. He pulled up in the wrap around driveway and pulled out his gun.

"Now, don't get out of here and think you going to do some slick shit. I promise you, Kiara. I will bust a cap in your no good ass."

"I know that now, but I never would have guessed that you could do me that way. Like I said before Daymion, I fucked up but I hope that after this you'll at least try to find it in your heart to forgive me."

"Yeah that ain't something I can promise. Now let's go."

Kiara led him up the steps and when she stuck her key in the lock, he put the gun to her back. She stiffened but proceeded to go inside, however, something different than what she'd been used to was in the air. The house was too quiet for her. She had always come into a television or a radio. Often times, Malachi would have his crew there playing video games or counting money but there had never been any peace.

"Malachi, I'm home. Where are you at?"

Day looked at her and wondered what was going on. He could tell that she had been thrown off by something but by what, he didn't know.

"What's wrong? Why you looking like that? Where the hell that nigga at?"

"I don't know, Daymion. Something is off."

About that time, Bones came in and as soon as Day saw him, he pointed his weapon. He couldn't afford to take any chances. He knew that the nigga that had walked in wasn't Malachi Jensen but he wondered what part he played in his organization.

"Who the fuck are you?"

"Yo man chill, I'm just the help."

Bones held his hands up high to show Day that he was not armed, but Day walked up to him and searched him anyway. He knew he couldn't take any chances. When he didn't find any weapons, he turned back to Kiara.

"Where that nigga at? Mufucka can't hide forever."

It wasn't Kiara that answered him, though. It was Bones.

"Malachi is gone. He left a few hours ago. Took his daughter with him but I can't tell you where they went. When he goes to his hideouts, he don't tell no one the location. Nigga changes phones and all so I can't even call him."

"What the hell do you mean he left? He couldn't have. There's no way he would leave me here like this. He's gotta be lying Daymion. His truck was in the driveway along with that little bitch's car. I knew she was bad news. I'm a kill that ho when I get my hands on her. Did he say when he was coming back?"

"No Kiara, he didn't but the last time he made a move like this I didn't see him again for months."

"That fucking bastard. I can't believe that he's done this to me. How could he do this? I kissed that motherfucker's ass and this is what he does to me in return."

Kiara could not believe her luck. She had gave up so much to be with Malachi and he had left her to fend for herself. She wasn't sure what she would do so she turned to Daymion.

"So, what now? You might as well go ahead and kill me because I can't help you. That little bitch came along and ever since, that is all he cares about. She's probably not even really his daughter. Fucking bitch probably lied about that."

"No Kiara, she's really his. Her mother was killed when she was younger. Never got to meet her father because his image had been tainted. Fuck nigga ain't deserve to be a father back then, and he damn sure don't deserve to be one now."

"You said her mother was killed, not that I really care but did they ever catch who did it? Did they even know who it was?"

"Yeah, they knew who did it but they won't ever get him."

"Who was it Daymion? Who killed that girl's mother."

He looked at her and answered. "It was me. I killed her."

Chapter 17

Time had passed slowly for Mellow, but it had finally come to an end. He couldn't have been happier when his cell door was rolled open and he was escorted handcuff free to the control room. Unlike Daymion, his first stop would be to a bitch. There was no place he would have rather been than balls deep in a wet pussy. He had been called the day before to classification and told that he would be emergency released the next day due to some type of error in his paperwork. He had thought about calling Day to pick him up but he decided to surprise him instead, but only after he got a nut.

"Alright Banks, get the hell out of here and don't bring your black ass back."

"Well damn, ain't y'all mufuckas 'pose to give me a ride or something. Maybe a fucking bus ticket. You can't expect me to walk. The shit hole is out here deep in the damn woods. Mufuckin crackas out here might lynch my ass. I can't walk down tha street."

"Man, get your ass out the door. Your ride is out front waiting on you."

"Yeah, aight. I knew that. Just wanted to make sure you bitches were paying attention."

When the door slid open, Mellow walked out and looked for the white state van but when he didn't see one waiting he became confused and turned around to go back in but a voice stopped him.

"Damn nigga, don't let me find out you trying to stay in that mufucka."

When he turned around and saw Daymion, he ran up and gave him a hug. He wasn't sure how he had found out about his release because Mellow himself had only found out the night before.

"How the hell did you know I was getting out? My release date should have been a few more months away."

"You thought I was gonna wait much longer to get my nigga out here with me? Hell nawl man. As soon as I got my paper right I pulled a few strings and here you go."

"Damn Day, thanks man but you gonna have to give me a few hours. A nigga like me needs a nut and until I get one I ain't gonna want to do shit else."

"Don't worry Mell, I already got you set up. Just get in and enjoy the ride. Let me handle everything else."

The two men got into the vehicle and enjoyed the smooth ride back to the city. Day pulled into the Hilton Hotel and parked. He opened his door and saw that Mellow didn't move and he wondered why.

"Nigga, let's go."

"Hell no, Day I ain't on none of that gay shit. I don't know what you got planned but I ain't going into no hotel room with another nigga."

"Bitch, don't try me and if I was gay, your ass would be the last one I'd want to go in. Now get your ass out, them hoes upstairs ain't gonna wait all night to bounce on some fresh dick."

Mellow finally got out and followed Day up to the Penthouse suite and was greeted by three women who had nothing on but an imagination. One was Asian and had hair to her ass. Her nipples hard as rocks and ready for him to kiss them. The white bitch had a short curly pixie cut with big blue eyes. He couldn't wait to look into while she sucked his children out of his nutsack and swallowed them down her throat. Her pussy had a small patch of hair that was shaped like a heart he couldn't wait to break. The dark skinned black girl had an ass so fat she should have been somewhere twerking. Her pussy was bare and her pearl peeked out between her fat lips. He couldn't wait to see if the berry really was sweeter. The three women walked up to him and began undressing him. He looked back at Day and mouthed a thank you and then Day closed the door and left him to enjoy the women all night long. The next day, he came back and picked Mellow up. It was time to get down to business."

"Sup man, I hope you enjoyed yourself."

"Aw Day, nigga them hoes sucked and fucked me dry. I may not ever be able to produce children because all my seeds went down that white bitch throat. And that Asian bitch was freaky as hell but all she wanted to do was lick my ass. Nigga, you know I don't play that back door shit. Oh yeah, and let me be frank and tell you that the juice is sweeter when the berry is darker. Thanks man, you hooked a nigga up fo' sho."

"No problem. Fucking with me you gonna always get what you want."

"Bet that. Right now though, I need to put some food in my stomach because pussy is good but that shit can't fill a nigga up."

Day drove them to his favorite restaurant where there was an all you can eat buffet and watched as Mellow filled his plate up. He was happy that he was able to get his friend free sooner than he had expected. He needed someone on his side because once again Valentine had disappeared.

"So, what you got planned for us to do, bruh? You know I'm ready to put in that work."

"And I'm ready for you to. I needed a loyal mufucka on my team, Mell. Shit ain't been right out here since I been home. Everybody I thought had my back ended up not having shit."

"Sorry 'bout that. Wish I could have been here to hold you down but I'm here now my nigga."

"Damn right."

The two grew silent for a second and enjoyed their food both with heavy minds. Mellow knew that Day had went through a lot of shit to get his son back so he wondered why he hadn't mentioned him.

"Yo dawg, what's up with ya son man? I know he used to be all you talked about but you ain't ever mentioned him. What's going on with that?"

"He got put down for a minute for a body. Bitch ass Kiara done ruined my kid man. He had to grow up before he was ready and that shit ain't right. Thought he was taking out Malachi but it ended up being one of his workers. My lil nigga's stuck until he's an adult. I been looking for Malachi ever since but his coward ass left town a while back. Ain't seen the nigga since."

"Damn Day, I'm sorry about that but what about his momma? Wasn't she fucking with that cat?"

"Hmm, yeah but that nigga dipped and left her ass dry. Found out he had a daughter and took her with him. Kiara thought we was gonna shake something together again but I'd rather cut my dick off than stick it up in that bitch again."

"You let that ho live man? After how she did your boy? Come on Day, she was supposed to eat a bullet. The fuck is wrong with you? Don't let me find out you done went soft, mufucka."

"Nah never that. Last I heard she was deep in the gutter sucking dick for crumbs. Ho don't mean shit to me."

"So what now? We gonna take shit over like we planned to do, or you got something better in mind. I'm ready to get that paper up so we can move big things. I ain't trying to deal with no small shit."

"Don't worry about that paper. We already got enough money and drugs to get started. I took all Malachi's shit trying to bring him out. Didn't work but my pockets got fat so we gonna use his shit to take over the rest of his shit. The whole town is ours now. Think you can hang with me?"

"Day, I was born for this shit. I don't mind working for you. Ain't nobody else I'd rather work for."

"Mellow my man, you ain't gonna work for me my nigga. We equal in this thang and ain't neither one of us greater than the other. You ya own boss just keep that shit loyal and we'll go a long way."

They gave each other dap and then finished their meals. When they were done, they decided to hit the blocks and start their reign of power. Those who had known him were glad that Daymion Myers was back in charge. Since he had been gone, the streets had been filled with greed and violence. Day believed in keeping the hood in unity. He figured the less drama going on, the more money would be made and everyone was on board.

Malachi's old workers were glad to put in time for Day and Mellow because they knew that they would finally be treated fairly. Day was back on top of the world and he couldn't have been more satisfied.

As time passed, him and Mellow's status did too and when jealousy reared its ugly head they were ready. The gang of six men ran in the stash house that Day had been chilling in but wasn't ready for what they ran up on. Day was sitting alone in the house without a care in the world and the men thought they would have it easy but little did they know that Day had already been tipped off and his soldiers were on standby.

"Get on the mufucking ground and don't move."

Day jumped up and did what they said. The money that he had been counting left lying on the table in neat stacks.

One of the men began picking it up and putting it in the bag they had brought while two others held guns to the back of Day's head. The other three ransacked the house but found nothing of value. Day and Mellow had moved the dope earlier that day. While the men were inside, his soldiers were outside surrounding the house getting ready to make their move.

The two men who stood over Day wasn't aware of the trap door that he was lying down on until he disappeared under the floor. Before they had a chance to react, their bodies were filled with bullets. All six men were killed and then the house was burned to the ground with them and the counterfeit money they had bagged up inside. After the attempted jack, no one else was bold enough to do the same and all things in the hood had went back to normal.

"Daymion. Daymion please talk to me."

He recognized Kiara's voice and although it had been a minute since he had heard it, he was still bothered by it. He had decided to spare her at the last minute because even though she had treated Dre poorly he didn't have the heart to kill his mother. Day couldn't look his son in the eyes and tell him that he had put a bullet in his mother's head. If his son wanted her dead, he would have to put in the work when he got out. Day had his status back so he knew that he'd be able to stop any heat from coming to his son in the event he pulled his trigger.

"Sup Kiara, what the hell you want? I thought I told you that I never wanted to see you again."

"Just listen to me please. I'm trying to make things right, Daymion. Dre will be getting out in a few years and I'd like to have my shit together in hopes that he will give me a chance to make things up to him. I admit that I was a horrible mother to him and yet, he never once condemned me for it. I'm tired of living the way that I'm living and hurting my son. I fucked up and the first rule of healing is admitting what you did wrong. Please help me, Daymion. Help me get back right."

"I don't know, Kiara. I think you've damaged Dre beyond repair. I'm not sure that he will ever let you back in."

"But it's worth a try. I started getting high after Malachi left me and that's not who I am. I have nothing and no one. I'm tired, Daymion. Please help me."

Day swore that he would never fuck with her again but how could he turn away from someone who was asking him for help. Kiara wasn't shit to him anymore but she was the one who gave life to his seed and for that he would forever be grateful.

"Aight. I'm a help you get back on your feet but that don't mean that anything will happen between us. I can't promise you that Dre is gonna give you the chance you asking for. That's his decision. Kiara, I spared you because you are his mother and I didn't want you to die by my hands but if he gives you another shot and you fuck him over, I won't stop him from coming for you. He ain't that kid you think he is. He's tarnished now and you're the reason. I can't protect you if it goes bad."

"I understand Daymion, but I have to at least try. Could you take me to see him?"

"See, now you asking for a bit much. I'm not sure he even wants to see you. He never even asks about you and I know that's a hard pill to swallow but it's the truth, you caused it on yourself so you can't be mad about it.

"I understand that I'm going to have to fight to gain his trust but I need you to talk to him. He will listen to you Day. You're his father and he will always look up to you."

"Hell no, you on your own with that like I already said."

"Okay, okay. Let me work on me first and then I'll try to go see him."

"Alright, but please don't make him promises you ain't gonna be able to keep. I gotta get out of here because I got shit to do. Holla at me when you ready to go to rehab and get the help you seeking. Don't call me for anything other than that."

Day turned around and started to walk away from her when the sound of a gunshot made him pull his weapon. He ran for cover and then looked around to see if he could figure out where the shot had come from. He wanted to see if another round would follow and after a few minutes he came back out in the open. He hadn't expected to be a target because ever since that jack at his stash house no one else had tried him. He would have known if there was another threat lurking in the shadows.

He quickly opened the door to his ride and jumped in. He picked up his phone and dialed Mellow's number but when he answered, Day was speechless. He couldn't get the words out because he was shocked at what he saw. He threw the phone down in the passenger seat and got back out. His eyes didn't deceive him although he wished that they had. The bullet hadn't been meant for him at all. The gunman had hit his target and it was over before they hit the ground. Kiara had asked for his help and he had agreed to help her but he had to eat those words because nothing could help her now.

Chapter 18

He watched close by as Kiara ran behind Daymion. He didn't know what they were saying but honestly, he really didn't care. They stood and talked longer than he had expected them to. Had the ex-couple made up for lost time or was he reading things wrong? He lit a cigarette and inhaled it hard into his lungs, a bad habit he had picked up and now one he couldn't quit. Since he had time, he decided to go ahead and put a bullet in the chamber. He would only need that one shot so why wasted time putting in more. He knew that he wouldn't miss because he had never done that before. He had a perfect aim even though it had been a while since he used it. She had betrayed him so she had to go. True enough, he had left in a hurry but he had planned to come back for her. She belonged to him and he wasn't about to let anyone else have her, especially him. He had his chance long ago and he blew it. He wouldn't get another one.

He had thought about killing him too but he wanted to be able to look him in the eyes when he took his last breath. He didn't want him to ever forget his face, so he would save him for next time, but it was her time now. He had known that one day she would be disloyal because it was in her blood. There was nothing he could do to change that but he still gave her a chance. She had been a nobody when he found her and he had turned her into something special. He treasured her but had a funny way of showing it. He had never learned to show anyone love so he did it the best way he could. Why didn't anyone understand that about him?

He watched as the man finally walked away and that was when he made his move. He aimed the gun and the red light shined bright on the spot he wanted to hit her heart. She didn't deserve to have one because she didn't know how to use it. When he pulled the trigger, he smiled as the bullet made contact and the red covered her torso. The anger he had for her poured out of the hole and she quickly dropped. The man ran for cover and pulled his weapon but he couldn't see him because he was like a shadow in the night. No matter which way he turned, he wouldn't notice him. However, he did notice her as she lie on the ground, dead and her soul already on the way to hell, a place she belonged in. The man couldn't save her and when he returned to get him, he wouldn't be able to save himself either.

He wasn't paying attention so he decided that it was a good time to leave and go back to where he had come from. He would continue to lay low until it was time to come back and take his shit from the mufucka that took it from him. What gave them the right to think that he would just let them have their way? No, he wanted what was his and he would get it by any means necessary.

Epilogue

Dre sat and watched the news, a daily routine he had become accustomed to. His mother's face showed on the screen looking back at him as if pleading for his forgiveness. However, he would never have the chance to tell her that he forgave her long ago. Scenes of the funeral were on every channel and each one had the same headline,

"Young woman gunned down in broad daylight. No motive as to why and no suspect."

Dre didn't care what the headline showed, he had known who the suspect was but he wouldn't hand him over to the police because he wanted to deal with it himself. That mufucka owed him and he would get his just due.

True enough, his mother had treated him like shit all of his life but she was the one who gave him life so he could never hate her.

Dre had become a mere shell of his former self. His heart stopped beating many years before. He lived on hatred now, a hatred so deep it would one day sink him but he didn't care because he felt like he had nothing else to live for.

He would do his time and then he would get out and handle what he had started. The job needed to be finished and he was the only one who could end it. Not his father and not anyone else. Just him. This shit was personal and hit close to home. He would take the rest of his time to get his mind right because he didn't want to make any mistakes. He would do what needed to be done to rid the streets of its garbage.

He would not only be a man when he got out but also, a force to be reckoned with, one that could not be tamed. A mufucka better watch they back because his knife would be cutting deep and when he pushed it in, he would not stop pushing until the bitch went all the way through.

Thug of Spades 3: Cemetery Gates

COMING SOON!

Lock Down Publications and Ca$h Presents
Assisted Publishing Packages

BASIC PACKAGE $499 Editing Cover Design Formatting	UPGRADED PACKAGE $800 Typing Editing Cover Design Formatting
ADVANCE PACKAGE $1,200 Typing Editing Cover Design Formatting Copyright registration Proofreading Upload book to Amazon	LDP SUPREME PACKAGE $1,500 Typing Editing Cover Design Formatting Copyright registration Proofreading Set up Amazon account Upload book to Amazon Advertise on LDP, Amazon and Facebook Page

***Other services available upon request.
Additional charges may apply

Lock Down Publications
P.O. Box 944
Stockbridge, GA 30281-9998
Phone: 470 303-9761

Submission Guideline

Submit the first three chapters of your completed manuscript to ldpsubmissions@gmail.com. In the subject line add **Your Book's Title**. The manuscript must be in a Word Doc file and sent as an attachment. Document should be in Times New Roman, double spaced, and in size 12 font. Also, provide your synopsis and full contact information. If sending multiple submissions, they must each be in a separate email.

Have a story but no way to send it electronically? You can still submit to LDP/Ca$h Presents. Send in the first three chapters, written or typed, of your completed manuscript to:

LDP: Submissions Dept
P.O. Box 944
Stockbridge, GA 30281-9998

DO NOT send original manuscript. Must be a duplicate. Provide your synopsis and a cover letter containing your full contact information.

Thanks for considering LDP and Ca$h Presents.

NEW RELEASES

BLOODLINE OF A SAVAGE **BY PRINCE A. TAUHID**

THE MURDER QUEENS 4 **BY MICHAEL GALLON**

THE BUTTERFLY MAFIA **BY FUMIYA PAYNE**

KING KILLA 2 **BY VINCENT "VITTO" HOLLOWAY**

BABY, I'M WINTERTIME COLD 3 **BY MEESHA**

THESE VICIOUS STREETS **BY PRINCE A. TAUHID**

TIL DEATH 2 **BY ARYANNA**

CITY OF SMOKE 2 **BY MOLOTTI**

STEPPERS **BY KING RIO**

THE LANE **BY KEN-KEN SPENCE**

MONEY GAME 2 **BY SMOOVE DOLLA**

THE BLACK DIAMOND CARTEL **BY SAYNOMORE**

CRIME BOSS 2 **BY PLAYA RAY**

THUG OF SPADES **BY COREY ROBINSON**

LOVE IN THE TRENCHES 2 **BY COREY ROBINSON**

TIL DEATH 3 **BY ARYANNA**

THE BIRTH OF A GANGSTER 4 **BY DELMONT PLAYER**

PRODUCT OF THE STREETS **BY DEMOND "MONEY" ANDERSON**

Coming Soon from Lock Down Publications/Ca$h Presents

BLOOD OF A BOSS VI
SHADOWS OF THE GAME II
TRAP BASTARD II
By **Askari**

LOYAL TO THE GAME IV
By **T.J. & Jelissa**

TRUE SAVAGE VIII
MIDNIGHT CARTEL IV
DOPE BOY MAGIC IV
CITY OF KINGZ III
NIGHTMARE ON SILENT AVE II
THE PLUG OF LIL MEXICO II
CLASSIC CITY II
By **Chris Green**

BLAST FOR ME III
A SAVAGE DOPEBOY III
CUTTHROAT MAFIA III
DUFFLE BAG CARTEL VII
HEARTLESS GOON VI
By **Ghost**

A HUSTLER'S DECEIT III
KILL ZONE II
BAE BELONGS TO ME III
TIL DEATH II
By **Aryanna**

KING OF THE TRAP III
By **T.J. Edwards**

GORILLAZ IN THE BAY V
3X KRAZY III
STRAIGHT BEAST MODE III
By **De'Kari**

KINGPIN KILLAZ IV
STREET KINGS III
PAID IN BLOOD III
CARTEL KILLAZ IV
DOPE GODS III
By **Hood Rich**

SINS OF A HUSTLA II
By **ASAD**

YAYO V
BRED IN THE GAME 2
By **S. Allen**

THE STREETS WILL TALK II
By **Yolanda Moore**

SON OF A DOPE FIEND III
HEAVEN GOT A GHETTO III
SKI MASK MONEY III
By **Renta**

LOYALTY AIN'T PROMISED III
By **Keith Williams**

QUIET MONEY IV
EXTENDED CLIP III
THUG LIFE IV
By **Trai'Quan**

THUG OF SPADES 2 | COREY ROBINSON

I'M NOTHING WITHOUT HIS LOVE II
SINS OF A THUG II
TO THE THUG I LOVED BEFORE II
IN A HUSTLER I TRUST II
By **Monet Dragun**

THE STREETS MADE ME IV
By **Larry D. Wright**

IF YOU CROSS ME ONCE III
ANGEL V
By **Anthony Fields**

THE STREETS WILL NEVER CLOSE IV
By **K'ajji**

HARD AND RUTHLESS III
KILLA KOUNTY IV
By **Khufu**

MONEY GAME III
By **Smoove Dolla**

MURDA WAS THE CASE III
Elijah R. Freeman

AN UNFORESEEN LOVE IV
BABY, I'M WINTERTIME COLD III
By **Meesha**

QUEEN OF THE ZOO III
By **Black Migo**

CONFESSIONS OF A JACKBOY III
By **Nicholas Lock**

JACK BOYS VS DOPE BOYS IV
A GANGSTA'S QUR'AN V
COKE GIRLZ II
COKE BOYS II
LIFE OF A SAVAGE V
CHI'RAQ GANGSTAS V
SOSA GANG III
BRONX SAVAGES II
BODYMORE KINGPINS II
By **Romell Tukes**

KING KILLA II
By **Vincent "Vitto" Holloway**

BETRAYAL OF A THUG III
By **Fre$h**

THE MURDER QUEENS III
By **Michael Gallon**

THE BIRTH OF A GANGSTER III
By **Delmont Player**

TREAL LOVE II
By **Le'Monica Jackson**

FOR THE LOVE OF BLOOD III
By **Jamel Mitchell**
RAN OFF ON DA PLUG II
By **Paper Boi Rari**

HOOD CONSIGLIERE III
By **Keese**

THUG OF SPADES 2 | COREY ROBINSON

PRETTY GIRLS DO NASTY THINGS II
By **Nicole Goosby**

PROTÉGÉ OF A LEGEND III
LOVE IN THE TRENCHES II
By **Corey Robinson**

IT'S JUST ME AND YOU II
By **Ah'Million**

FOREVER GANGSTA III
By **Adrian Dulan**

GORILLAZ IN THE TRENCHES II
By **SayNoMore**

THE COCAINE PRINCESS VIII
By **King Rio**

CRIME BOSS II
By **Playa Ray**

LOYALTY IS EVERYTHING III
By **Molotti**

HERE TODAY GONE TOMORROW II
By **Fly Rock**

REAL G'S MOVE IN SILENCE II
By **Von Diesel**

GRIMEY WAYS IV
By **Ray Vinci**

Available Now

RESTRAINING ORDER I & II
By **CA$H & Coffee**

LOVE KNOWS NO BOUNDARIES I II & III
By **Coffee**

RAISED AS A GOON I, II, III & IV
BRED BY THE SLUMS I, II, III
BLAST FOR ME I & II
ROTTEN TO THE CORE I II III
A BRONX TALE I, II, III
DUFFLE BAG CARTEL I II III IV V VI
HEARTLESS GOON I II III IV V
A SAVAGE DOPEBOY I II
DRUG LORDS I II III
CUTTHROAT MAFIA I II
KING OF THE TRENCHES
By **Ghost**

LAY IT DOWN I & II
LAST OF A DYING BREED I II
BLOOD STAINS OF A SHOTTA I & II III
By **Jamaica**

LOYAL TO THE GAME I II III
LIFE OF SIN I, II III
By **TJ & Jelissa**

IF LOVING HIM IS WRONG...I & II
LOVE ME EVEN WHEN IT HURTS I II III
By **Jelissa**

BLOODY COMMAS I & II
SKI MASK CARTEL I, II & III
KING OF NEW YORK I II, III IV V
RISE TO POWER I II III
COKE KINGS I II III IV V
BORN HEARTLESS I II III IV
KING OF THE TRAP I II
By **T.J. Edwards**

WHEN THE STREETS CLAP BACK I & II III
THE HEART OF A SAVAGE I II III IV
MONEY MAFIA I II
LOYAL TO THE SOIL I II III
By **Jibril Williams**

A DISTINGUISHED THUG STOLE MY HEART I II &
III
LOVE SHOULDN'T HURT I II III IV
RENEGADE BOYS I II III IV
PAID IN KARMA I II III
SAVAGE STORMS I II III
AN UNFORESEEN LOVE I II III
BABY, I'M WINTERTIME COLD I II
By **Meesha**

A GANGSTER'S CODE I &, II III
A GANGSTER'S SYN I II III
THE SAVAGE LIFE I II III
CHAINED TO THE STREETS I II III
BLOOD ON THE MONEY I II III
A GANGSTA'S PAIN I II III
By **J-Blunt**

PUSH IT TO THE LIMIT
By **Bre' Hayes**

THUG OF SPADES 2 | COREY ROBINSON

BLOOD OF A BOSS I, II, III, IV, V
SHADOWS OF THE GAME
TRAP BASTARD
By **Askari**

THE STREETS BLEED MURDER I, II & III
THE HEART OF A GANGSTA I II& III
By **Jerry Jackson**

CUM FOR ME I II III IV V VI VII VIII
An **LDP Erotica Collaboration**

BRIDE OF A HUSTLA I II & II
THE FETTI GIRLS I, II& III
CORRUPTED BY A GANGSTA I, II III, IV
BLINDED BY HIS LOVE
THE PRICE YOU PAY FOR LOVE I, II ,III
DOPE GIRL MAGIC I II III
By **Destiny Skai**

WHEN A GOOD GIRL GOES BAD
By **Adrienne**

TRUE SAVAGE I II III IV V VI VII
DOPE BOY MAGIC I, II, III
MIDNIGHT CARTEL I II III
CITY OF KINGZ I II
NIGHTMARE ON SILENT AVE
THE PLUG OF LIL MEXICO II
CLASSIC CITY
By **Chris Green**

THE COST OF LOYALTY I II III
By Kweli

A GANGSTER'S REVENGE I II III & IV
THE BOSS MAN'S DAUGHTERS I II III IV V
A SAVAGE LOVE I & II
BAE BELONGS TO ME I II
A HUSTLER'S DECEIT I, II, III
WHAT BAD BITCHES DO I, II, III
SOUL OF A MONSTER I II III
KILL ZONE
A DOPE BOY'S QUEEN I II III
TIL DEATH
By **Aryanna**

A KINGPIN'S AMBITION
A KINGPIN'S AMBITION **II**
I MURDER FOR THE DOUGH
By **Ambitious**

A DOPEBOY'S PRAYER
By **Eddie "Wolf" Lee**

THE KING CARTEL I, II & III
By **Frank Gresham**

THESE NIGGAS AIN'T LOYAL I, II & III
By **Nikki Tee**

GANGSTA SHYT I II &III
By **CATO**

THE ULTIMATE BETRAYAL
By **Phoenix**

BOSS'N UP I, II & III
By **Royal Nicole**

THUG OF SPADES 2 | COREY ROBINSON

I LOVE YOU TO DEATH
By **Destiny J**

I RIDE FOR MY HITTA
I STILL RIDE FOR MY HITTA
By **Misty Holt**

LOVE & CHASIN' PAPER
By **Qay Crockett**

TO DIE IN VAIN
SINS OF A HUSTLA
By **ASAD**

BROOKLYN HUSTLAZ
By **Boogsy Morina**

BROOKLYN ON LOCK I & II
By **Sonovia**

GANGSTA CITY
By **Teddy Duke**

A DRUG KING AND HIS DIAMOND I & II III
A DOPEMAN'S RICHES
HER MAN, MINE'S TOO I, II
CASH MONEY HO'S
THE WIFEY I USED TO BE I II
PRETTY GIRLS DO NASTY THINGS
By Nicole Goosby

STEADY MOBBN' I, II, III
THE STREETS STAINED MY SOUL I II III
By **Marcellus Allen**
199

LIPSTICK KILLAH I, II, III
CRIME OF PASSION I II & III
FRIEND OR FOE I II III
By **Mimi**

TRAPHOUSE KING I II & III
KINGPIN KILLAZ I II III
STREET KINGS I II
PAID IN BLOOD I II
CARTEL KILLAZ I II III
DOPE GODS I II
By **Hood Rich**

STEADY MOBBN' I, II, III
THE STREETS STAINED MY SOUL I II III
By **Marcellus Allen**

WHO SHOT YA I, II, III
SON OF A DOPE FIEND I II
HEAVEN GOT A GHETTO I II
SKI MASK MONEY I II
By **Renta**

GORILLAZ IN THE BAY I II III IV
TEARS OF A GANGSTA I II
3X KRAZY I II
STRAIGHT BEAST MODE I II
By **DE'KARI**

TRIGGADALE I II III
MURDA WAS THE CASE I II
By **Elijah R. Freeman**

THE STREETS ARE CALLING
By **Duquie Wilson**

SLAUGHTER GANG I II III
RUTHLESS HEART I II III
By **Willie Slaughter**

GOD BLESS THE TRAPPERS I, II, III
THESE SCANDALOUS STREETS I, II, III
FEAR MY GANGSTA I, II, III IV, V
THESE STREETS DON'T LOVE NOBODY I, II
BURY ME A G I, II, III, IV, V
A GANGSTA'S EMPIRE I, II, III, IV
THE DOPEMAN'S BODYGAURD I II
THE REALEST KILLAZ I II III
THE LAST OF THE OGS I II III
By **Tranay Adams**

MARRIED TO A BOSS I II III
By **Destiny Skai & Chris Green**

KINGZ OF THE GAME I II III IV V VI VII
CRIME BOSS
By **Playa Ray**

FUK SHYT
By **Blakk Diamond**

DON'T F#CK WITH MY HEART I II
By **Linnea**

ADDICTED TO THE DRAMA I II III
IN THE ARM OF HIS BOSS II
By **Jamila**

LOYALTY AIN'T PROMISED I II
By **Keith Williams**

YAYO I II III IV
A SHOOTER'S AMBITION I II
BRED IN THE GAME
By **S. Allen**

TRAP GOD I II III
RICH $AVAGE I II III
MONEY IN THE GRAVE I II III
By **Martell Troublesome Bolden**

FOREVER GANGSTA I II
GLOCKS ON SATIN SHEETS I II
By **Adrian Dulan**

TOE TAGZ I II III IV
LEVELS TO THIS SHYT I II
IT'S JUST ME AND YOU
By **Ah'Million**

KINGPIN DREAMS I II III
RAN OFF ON DA PLUG
By **Paper Boi Rari**

CONFESSIONS OF A GANGSTA I II III IV
CONFESSIONS OF A JACKBOY I II
By **Nicholas Lock**

I'M NOTHING WITHOUT HIS LOVE
SINS OF A THUG
TO THE THUG I LOVED BEFORE
A GANGSTA SAVED XMAS
IN A HUSTLER I TRUST
By **Monet Dragun**

THE STREETS MADE ME I II III
By **Larry D. Wright**

QUIET MONEY I II III
THUG LIFE I II III
EXTENDED CLIP I II
A GANGSTA'S PARADISE
By **Trai'Quan**

CAUGHT UP IN THE LIFE I II III
THE STREETS NEVER LET GO I II III
By **Robert Baptiste**

NEW TO THE GAME I II III
MONEY, MURDER & MEMORIES I II III
By **Malik D. Rice**

CREAM I II III
THE STREETS WILL TALK
By **Yolanda Moore**

LIFE OF A SAVAGE I II III IV
A GANGSTA'S QUR'AN I II III IV
MURDA SEASON I II III
GANGLAND CARTEL I II III
CHI'RAQ GANGSTAS I II III IV
KILLERS ON ELM STREET I II III
JACK BOYZ N DA BRONX I II III
A DOPEBOY'S DREAM I II III
JACK BOYS VS DOPE BOYS I II III
COKE GIRLZ
COKE BOYS
SOSA GANG I II
BRONX SAVAGES
BODYMORE KINGPINS
By **Romell Tukes**

CONCRETE KILLA I II III
VICIOUS LOYALTY I II III
By **Kingpen**

THE ULTIMATE SACRIFICE I, II, III, IV, V, VI
KHADIFI
IF YOU CROSS ME ONCE I II
ANGEL I II III IV
IN THE BLINK OF AN EYE
By **Anthony Fields**

THE LIFE OF A HOOD STAR
By **Ca$h & Rashia Wilson**

THE STREETS WILL NEVER CLOSE I II III
By **K'ajji**

NIGHTMARES OF A HUSTLA I II III
By **King Dream**

HARD AND RUTHLESS I II
MOB TOWN 251
THE BILLIONAIRE BENTLEYS I II III
REAL G'S MOVE IN SILENCE
By **Von Diesel**

GHOST MOB
By **Stilloan Robinson**

MOB TIES I II III IV V VI
SOUL OF A HUSTLER, HEART OF A KILLER I II
GORILLAZ IN THE TRENCHES
By **SayNoMore**

KILLA KOUNTY I II III IV
By Khufu

BODYMORE MURDERLAND I II III
THE BIRTH OF A GANGSTER I II
By **Delmont Player**

FOR THE LOVE OF A BOSS
By **C. D. Blue**

MOBBED UP I II III IV
THE BRICK MAN I II III IV V
THE COCAINE PRINCESS I II III IV V VI VII
By **King Rio**

MONEY GAME I II
By **Smoove Dolla**

A GANGSTA'S KARMA I II III
By **FLAME**

KING OF THE TRENCHES I II III
By **GHOST & TRANAY ADAMS**

QUEEN OF THE ZOO I II
By **Black Migo**

GRIMEY WAYS I II III
By **Ray Vinci**

XMAS WITH AN ATL SHOOTER
By **Ca$h & Destiny Skai**

PROTÉGÉ OF A LEGEND I II
LOVE IN THE TRENCHES
By **Corey Robinson**

KING KILLA
By **Vincent "Vitto" Holloway**

BETRAYAL OF A THUG I II
By **Fre$h**

THE MURDER QUEENS I II
By **Michael Gallon**

TREAL LOVE
By **Le'Monica Jackson**

FOR THE LOVE OF BLOOD I II
By **Jamel Mitchell**

HOOD CONSIGLIERE I II
By **Keese**

BORN IN THE GRAVE I II III
By **Self Made Tay**

MOAN IN MY MOUTH
By **XTASY**

TORN BETWEEN A GANGSTER AND A
GENTLEMAN
By **J-BLUNT & Miss Kim**

LOYALTY IS EVERYTHING I II
By **Molotti**

HERE TODAY GONE TOMORROW
By **Fly Rock**

PILLOW PRINCESS
By **S. Hawkins**

SANCTIFIED AND HORNY
by **XTASY**

THE PLUG OF LIL MEXICO 2
by **CHRIS GREEN**

THE BLACK DIAMOND CARTEL
by **SAYNOMORE**

THE BIRTH OF A GANGSTER 3
by **DELMONT PLAYER**

BOOKS BY LDP'S CEO, CA$H

TRUST IN NO MAN
TRUST IN NO MAN 2
TRUST IN NO MAN 3
BONDED BY BLOOD
SHORTY GOT A THUG
THUGS CRY
THUGS CRY 2
THUGS CRY 3
TRUST NO BITCH
TRUST NO BITCH 2
TRUST NO BITCH 3
TIL MY CASKET DROPS
RESTRAINING ORDER
RESTRAINING ORDER 2
IN LOVE WITH A CONVICT
LIFE OF A HOOD STAR
XMAS WITH AN ATL SHOOTER

www.ingramcontent.com/pod-product-compliance
Lightning Source LLC
Chambersburg PA
CBHW071159260626
47162CB00003B/1112